Midwives On-Call at Christmas

*Mothers, midwives and mistletoe—
lives changing for ever at Christmas!*

Welcome to Cambridge Royal Hospital—
and to the exceptional midwives
who make up its special Maternity Unit!

They deliver tiny bundles of joy on a daily
basis, but Christmas really is a time for
miracles—as midwives Bonnie, Hope,
Jessica and Isabel are about to find out.

Amidst the drama and emotion of babies
arriving at all hours of the day and night,
these midwives still find time for some
sizzling romance under the mistletoe!

This holiday season, don't miss the festive,
heartwarming spin-off to the dazzling
Midwives On-Call continuity
from Mills & Boon Medical Romance:

A Touch of Christmas Magic
by Scarlet Wilson

Her Christmas Baby Bump
by Robin Gianna

Playboy Doc's Mistletoe Kiss
by Tina Beckett

Her Doctor's Christmas Proposal
by Louisa George

All available now!

Dear Reader,

I love Christmas. I love the decorated trees and the coloured lights and all the yummy scents that go along with the holiday. So when I was asked to take part in Midwives On-Call at Christmas, I jumped at the chance. And I'm glad I did. I had so much fun with this story. My characters were all I could have hoped for, and I even sneaked a sprig of mistletoe into one of the scenes. Absolutely romantic!

Thank you for joining Jess and Dean as they make their way through this festive season and tackle some serious issues (all the while treating the tiniest and most adorable patients). Maybe they'll even share a kiss or two under that mistletoe...

I hope you enjoy their story as much as I loved writing it.

Love,

Tina Beckett

PLAYBOY DOC'S MISTLETOE KISS

BY
TINA BECKETT

First published in Great Britain 2015
by Mills & Boon, an imprint of Harlequin (UK) Limited,
Eton House, 18-24 Paradise Road, Richmond, Surrey, TW9 1SR

© 2015 Harlequin Books S.A.

Special thanks and acknowledgement are given to Tina Beckett for her
contribution to the Midwives On-Call at Christmas series

ISBN: 978-0-263-26060-1

Harlequin (UK) Limited's policy is to use papers that are natural,
renewable and recyclable products and made from wood grown in
sustainable forests. The logging and manufacturing processes conform
to the legal environmental regulations of the country of origin.

Printed and bound in Great Britain
by CPI Antony Rowe, Chippenham, Wiltshire

A three-time Golden Heart finalist, **Tina Beckett** is the product of a Navy upbringing. Fortunately she found someone who enjoys travelling just as much as she does and married him! Having lived in Brazil for many years, Tina is fluent in Portuguese and loves to use that beautiful country as a backdrop for many of her stories. When not writing or visiting far-flung places Tina enjoys riding horses, hiking with her family and hanging out on Facebook and Twitter.

Books by Tina Beckett

Mills & Boon Medical Romance

Hot Brazilian Docs!
To Play With Fire
The Dangers of Dating Dr Carvalho

One Night That Changed Everything
NYC Angels: Flirting with Danger
The Lone Wolf's Craving
Doctor's Guide to Dating in the Jungle
Her Hard to Resist Husband
His Girl From Nowhere
How to Find a Man in Five Dates
The Soldier She Could Never Forget
Her Playboy's Secret
Hot Doc from Her Past

Visit the Author Profile page
at millsandboon.co.uk for more titles.

To my husband,
who is willing to drop whatever he's doing
to sip hot cocoa and stare at the Christmas lights with me.
I love you, honey!

Praise for Tina Beckett

'...a tension-filled emotional story with just the right
amount of drama. The author's vivid description of the
Brazilian jungle and its people make this story something
special.'

—*RT Book Reviews* on
Doctor's Guide to Dating in the Jungle

'Mills & Boon Medical Romance lovers will definitely
like *NYC Angels: Flirting with Danger* by Tina Beckett—
for who *doesn't* like a good forbidden romance?'

—*HarlequinJunkie*

CHAPTER ONE

JESSICA ANN BLACK was used to chaos. As she arrived at her fifth case of the day—a home birth—that was exactly what she found. Chaos.

Daphne's birthing coach—who was also her husband—was on the ground beside the bed, out of commission. The woman's mum was doing her best to calm her daughter, but the shaky voice and panicked expression said she was in over her head.

Taking a deep breath, Jess waded into the fray, her training kicking in. A senior midwife at Cambridge Royal Hospital, she wasn't called out to many home births, but she'd followed Daphne through two successful deliveries in as many years. When she'd begged Jess to see to this one as well, she hadn't had the heart to refuse. All had gone well with the other two, so she'd expected the same with the third.

Except it wasn't.

Daphne gripped the bed, panting in quick breaths. Hurrying over to her, Jess gave her mum's shoulder a gentle squeeze and asked her to see to Daphne's husband. Then she focused all her attention on her patient.

"I'm going to check you, love. Give me just a moment." Snapping on her gloves to measure her patient's dilation, she found instead the baby had crowned—head pressed tight against her fingertips.

Alarm bells flashed through her system, but she suppressed them. Jess had learned to school her features into bland indifference—no matter what she was faced with. So much so that the hospital often asked her to step in when there was a particularly tense or emotional situation. She somehow had the ability to defuse them.

Maybe because she had plenty of practice doing just that in her own family. Especially with her sister. Only it didn't always work, as she'd learned the hard way.

"How long have you been like this?" Jess grabbed several towels from the stack of clean ones Daphne had readied at her bedside and laid them just below the woman's bum.

"Hours." The word was accompanied by another moan.

Since Jess had only gotten the call fifteen minutes ago, she knew that wasn't true, but it probably did seem like hours to someone who was scared and alone. Well, she wasn't alone, but she might as well be.

This baby was coming much faster than the others had. Jess had left the hospital as soon as Daphne's husband rang her, but somewhere between then and now things had taken a turn, and Rick had fainted dead away. No wonder he'd panicked. Jess had always been here for this part of the delivery. He'd probably locked his knees and sent his blood pressure plummeting until he passed out.

She prayed the baby was still okay.

"You know how to do this by heart, Daphne. Your baby is almost here, so I need you to grab your legs and bear down on your bottom."

More panting. "I don't know if I can. Hurts so much more than the others."

Jess didn't stop to ask where the other two children

were; hopefully they were with someone and not wandering around the house alone. She'd tackle that problem after she handled this one.

If she was good at one thing, it was taking things as they came at her—dealing with one task at a time in the order of urgency. And right now, they needed to get this baby out.

"You can do it, love, absolutely you can." She helped Daphne get into position and told her to wait for the next contraction and then push. Jess's phone was on the table next to her, the hospital's number already on the screen ready to be dialed at the touch of a button.

"It's here." Daphne groaned...or maybe the sound came from her husband, Jess wasn't sure, but her patient began bearing down as Jess counted in slow measured tones.

"Perfect. Take a breath and push again."

The baby's head slowly emerged, the characteristic shape from compression very much evident in this little one, which made her again wonder how long he or she had been stuck in the birth canal.

As soon as she delivered the baby's head, she instructed her patient to stop, while she continued to support the neck and prepared for the hardest part of the delivery: the shoulders.

Daphne had buckled down to work, her earlier panic gone as she concentrated on the job at hand.

"Okay, let's go at it again."

The first shoulder appeared, and Jess maneuvered it, easing it out. Then came the second. A little rotation to the left. There! Both were out. "One more good push, Daphne, and we should have it."

Out of the corner of her eye, she saw the woman's mother guiding Daphne's husband to a nearby chair. She called over, "Rick, put your head between your knees. Daphne is doing fine."

Her patient pushed again and, as she'd suspected, the baby—a girl—slipped right out and into her waiting hands. The newborn cried without any stimulation, making Jess go slack with relief.

"You've got a baby girl. Congratulations." Still holding the newborn, she used the tips of her fingers to pick another towel and draped it over Daphne's chest. She then placed the baby on it. "Love on her for a minute, while I cut the cord."

With no one to hand her any instruments, she reached into her bag and found clamps and scissors in sterile packages and ripped them open. She then clamped and cut the cord and delivered the afterbirth.

As soon as everyone was stable, and Rick was back on his feet and standing beside his wife looking rather sheepish, she pressed the dial button on her mobile. Daphne and the baby would need to be checked.

Expecting one of the nurses to answer, she tensed for a second when a low masculine drawl brushed across her ear. "Cambridge Royal Hospital, Dean Edwards here."

Dean Edwards. Special Care Baby Unit doctor and one of the hospital's most eligible bachelors. Definitely its most notorious from all of the whispered love-'em-and-leave-'em tales that floated through the hospital's corridors.

Forcing her voice to remain absolutely level and calm even though her pulse had rocketed through the roof, she informed him of the situation and that she was arranging for transport to take the family to hospital. She asked that someone be there to meet them when they arrived.

"Will you be arriving with them?"

She hesitated, tempted for some strange reason to say

yes. Shaking herself free of the urge, she said, "I have somewhere else to be, but I'll make sure they get off without any problems."

"I'll be waiting." The words sent a strange shiver through her. Almost as if he'd be waiting for her.

Ridiculous. Back to reality, Jess.

She still had her mum and dad's anniversary party to get through as soon as she left here. The last thing she needed was to be mooning over Dean Edwards. Besides, she needed all her wits about her, because the party meant she would be facing her twin sister, who she'd only seen a handful of times since Abbie's wedding day.

The day Abbie had married Jess's fiancé.

"You're still after him aren't you? You'd love it if something happened and we broke up."

Jess stood there in shock as her sister's furious words poured over her.

After him? The familiar accusation ripped open old wounds and laid them bare.

Hadn't it been the other way around six years ago? Martin had been Jess's fiancé, until Abbie—just like with everything else—had decided she wanted what her sister had.

"Just stop it, Abbie. I'm not up to it tonight." The pounding in her temples attested to that fact.

"Well, that's too bad. Because I have a few things I want to get off my chest, and since we're both here…"

Jess took a breath and reminded herself that they were at their parents' thirtieth anniversary party and that her sister was seven months pregnant with her fourth child. Throwing another brick on the restraining wall that held back her own bitter feelings, she tried again.

"Let's not fight, Abbie." She made her voice as calm

as possible, trying to ward off the inevitable. "This isn't the time or place."

"Who's fighting? Certainly not me."

"No? It sure sounds like it. Those text messages weren't from me. Did you ever think about ringing the number, or asking Martin directly?"

Her sister had basically accused her of sexting her husband while he was away on business trips. It was ludicrous to have to defend herself against such a ridiculous accusation. Besides, she couldn't imagine Martin being stupid enough to leave incriminating texts on his phone for Abbie to find. There had to be another explanation. Unfortunately, Martin was away on yet another trip.

"I'm asking *you*, instead." Her sister's thunderous expression made her take a step back.

"You can well and truly have him, Abbie. I don't want him back."

It was on the tip of her tongue to say that she'd found someone else—that she was madly in love. But she didn't. Because there was no one even on the horizon. Madly or otherwise.

She hadn't gone out on a date in ages.

"Oh, really?" Her sister put a hand to her belly, disbelief written all over her face. "Well, you'd better make sure it stays that way."

Jess's teeth ground together, her anger rising. "That's enough."

"I still have a few things to make perfectly clear."

This was why she avoided being in the same room as her twin, going so far as to move from London to Cambridge. Those five minutes in the birthing suite—when her sister had arrived first—had set a pattern that continued to this day. Abbie had to be first in everything. Or at least look like it. She'd excelled at everything she touched, outdoing Jess whenever she got the chance. Her sister had even followed her to uni and studied midwifery, going one step further and making it look as if she'd had the idea first.

Abbie had the home and the family her mum had always wanted both her girls to have. Another source of contention, since her parents felt Jess poured too much of herself into her career.

But she loved her job. She wasn't substituting one thing for another. Nor was she worried about her biological clock running out.

She lowered her voice, aware that her mum was now looking at them from across the room with a frown. Time to put a stop to this. "This isn't a competition. It never was."

"You think I'm competing? With *you*?" Her sister took a step closer, crowding Jess against the buffet table, ignoring the guest who tiptoed around them, plate in hand. "Believe me, you'd know it if I were."

The problem was, Jess did know it. It was the reason she'd had little to do with her sister since agreeing to be her maid of honor—the day Martin had stood at the front of the congregation and watched the bridesmaids glide down the aisle of the church. He'd spared her hardly a glance—eyes only for Abbie. That had been one of the worst nights of her life. Her sister had gloated openly, even as she'd claimed to be glad to leave behind her aspirations of becoming a midwife. Martin and Abbie's first child was born seven months later. She'd been "blissfully happy" ever since.

"Listen, Abbie, if I were going to send sexy texts to someone, it certainly wouldn't be to Martin."

"What is that supposed to mean?"

More anger flared inside of her. She couldn't believe her

sister was doing this at their parents' party. They'd come all the way to Cambridge from their home in London just so Jess could attend—her crazy hours leaving her little time for holidays or anything else. Leave it to Abbie to try to ruin their efforts by thinking of no one but herself. Well, this time, Jess was going to call her on it.

The restraining wall she had so carefully erected burst at the seams, allowing words she'd vowed never to say to spew out in a rush.

"What I mean is Martin's gone a little soft around the middle, hasn't he? Besides, have you ever heard the expression *once a cheater always a cheater*?"

Her sister flushed bright red. "I can't believe you just said that. Martin loved me. What were we supposed to do?"

Jess could think of a few things, but the pain behind her eyes was growing, warning her that things were about to get much worse. The last thing she wanted to do was burst into tears in front of her sister.

She slid to the side to get away from Abbie and from her own growing frustration. "Okay, I'm done. This is *not* the place to be sniping at each other."

"Sniping? Why, you…" Abbie clutched her stomach with both hands.

Jess rolled her eyes. Whenever challenged by anyone—her parents, her friends, her sister—Abbie always felt dizzy, or sick…or too exhausted to "have this conversation".

"Let's just call a truce and go back to our own sides of the room, okay?"

"I think—" Her sister moaned. "I think something's wrong with the baby."

She suddenly realized all the color had leached from Abbie's face. Her sister had also reached out to grip the table, knocking over a tiered set of plates that held expensive hors d'oeuvres.

Crash!

The china exploded on the ground spraying tiny crab cakes and stuffed mushrooms in every direction.

The whole room went silent, all eyes coming to rest on the twins. Jess's anger transformed to horror.

Because Abbie wasn't acting or trying to garner sympathy. Jess recognized the signs enough to know her sister was in labor.

And the baby was two months early.

CHAPTER TWO

SHE'D BEEN HERE for hours.

Dean Edwards had popped into Cambridge Royal's Special Care Baby Unit five times since his shift started to check on his tiny charges, and each time he'd spied her standing in almost the exact same spot with her shoulder propped against the wall staring at the row of cots.

Dressed in a red party frock that hugged her slender frame, she'd obviously come from some kind of celebration. Only she wasn't celebrating now.

In fact, she looked devastated, as if the baby she hovered over had passed away. But although tiny, the newborn was very much alive. And right now, those bloodshot eyes and tracks of mascara were doing a number on his gut, and he didn't like it.

Not much got to him in his thirty-five years. Except a woman crying. It brought back memories of unhappy times and unhappy people.

He'd been willing to let her stand there as he worked, but the increasing tightness in his throat finally drove him to clear it and cross over to her.

"She's going to be okay, you know." He kept his voice low and soothing, partly to avoid startling the sleeping babies and partly to keep her from realizing how her obvious grief had affected him.

She didn't even glance in his direction. "It's my fault she's here in the first place."

That made him frown. "Sometimes these things just happen."

"Do they?"

Light brown wounded eyes swung to meet his and the punch to his midsection was nothing like that earlier uneasiness.

"Yes." He leaned his shoulder against the same wall so that their faces would be level with each other. Long and lean, she was still a head shorter than he was. "And you need to get some rest. You can't do her any good, if you're exhausted."

Her eyes closed for a minute and her chest rose and fell before she looked at him again. "I'm not her mother."

Those words made his frown deepen. Had he detected a wistful note in her voice? "I know who you are."

"I'm Jessica…" She blinked, arms wrapping around her waist. "You do?"

Why so surprised? They'd spoken on the phone earlier today.

"Did you think you were invisible or something? If so, you should know—" he leaned in closer and lowered his voice to a conspiratorial whisper "—your invisibility cloak might need recharging."

That was the truth, because with her long blonde hair, soft caring eyes and a laugh that could melt the hardest of hearts, there was no way he could have missed noticing her from the moment she'd started working at the hospital. And because of that, he'd done his damnedest to avoid her. Until now. When he couldn't.

A trace of a smile appeared on her face. "Really? Because most times, I pretty much feel… Scratch that." She stood upright with a shrug. "Sometimes people confuse me with my sister. We do look quite alike."

The sister?

He'd seen her. Had been there right after her baby was born. And while there were obvious similarities in coloring and bone structure, that ended when you looked beyond, to what was inside. Maybe her sister's frown lines were due to worry about her child, but Dean didn't think so. Because Jessica's brows were smooth and clear. The only lines she had were little crinkles at the far corners of her eyes that spoke of smiles and laughter.

"Do you think so?" he asked. "Because I'm just not seeing it."

Up went delicate brows. "We're twins. *Identical* twins."

He couldn't stop himself from poking at what was evidently a sore spot. This woman revealed a lot about herself without saying much at all. "So you're saying not even your mother could tell you apart?"

"Of course she could, it's just that..." Another quick breath. "Some people can't."

Dean glanced at the babies across from him, a rare moment when they were still all snoozing away, the clicking of ventilators and beeping machinery the only sounds in the room besides the two of them. He'd like to keep it that way, if possible. These little ones needed rest. Lots of it. They weren't the only ones. Jessica Black looked well and truly exhausted, so much so that he was surprised she was still standing. She needed to take a break.

Against his better judgement, Dean was going to suggest she do just that.

"Have you been home yet?"

She shook her head, still staring at the cots. "I don't want to leave."

"I know, but you look like you could use some downtime—I know I could. Do you want to go somewhere and grab a bite? My treat."

Something about the way she'd blamed herself for her niece's premature birth made him want to find out why she would think something like that. The time he'd seen her sister beside the baby's incubator had given him pause. Jess had been there as well, but the sisters hadn't spoken a word to each other. In fact, the chill in the room had been almost palpable.

Instead of nodding or politely turning him down, Jess blinked. "Excuse me?"

Not quite the reaction he'd expected. "I was asking if you wanted to get something to eat."

"I heard what you said."

Okay, so coming over here to comfort her was evidently the wrong choice. She didn't seem to want it. Any of it.

Since he'd already asked, though, what choice did he have except to see this through to the bitter end?

"So, is that a yes? Or a no?"

"Oh, it's definitely a no. Not interested." She shook her head. "I may look like her, but I'm definitely *not* her. And your timing, by the way, is lousy."

Timing?

Bloody hell. Did she think he was trying to hit on her because she looked like her sister? If so, this day was just getting better and better. He'd heard bits and pieces of enough conversations to know that he had a reputation. An undeserved one. He was squeaky clean as far as keeping his professional life separate from his private. Beyond that, though, all bets were off.

He forced himself to glance at his watch and give her an easy grin, even as his back molars ground against each other. "Really? Because where I come from, timing is everything. And *this* is the time I normally eat supper. Not go to bed."

There were several seconds of absolute silence. When she looked at him again, her cheeks bloomed with red.

Maybe he should soften his words a little. "I promise this is about sitting down to a meal and giving yourself a much-needed break. Nothing else."

"Oh, Lord." She tipped her head back against the wall and closed her eyes. "I'm sorry. I just…I thought…"

Yeah, sweetheart. I know exactly what you thought. And she was partially right. With a roomful of sick babies, and after a particularly exhausting shift, bed was exactly where his mind was heading.

As in falling into it. To sleep. By himself.

"Supper," he confirmed. "I'll stay on my side of the table the whole time."

If anything, her color deepened. "It's been a difficult day. It was my parents' anniversary. And with Abbie going into labor in the middle of it, I'm not thinking straight."

All my fault.

Wasn't that what she'd said when he first came over to talk to her?

Suddenly he wanted to know why she blamed herself. "Which is why you need to get away for a bit. I know a great little place just around the corner that serves wonderful Indian cuisine. And it leans a bit to the fancy side, so you won't be overdressed." He allowed the side of his mouth to kick up again to reassure her.

She didn't smile back. Instead, her glance went to her dress and then back toward the row of special-care cots. "Are you sure she'll be okay?"

Instead of answering her, and since he couldn't give her any long-term prognosis at the moment, Dean took his stethoscope from around his neck and dropped it into his pocket. After washing his hands, he went over to the baby's incubator. He could feel Jess's eyes on him the whole time as he slid his hands through the holes on the side of the bed and stroked a tiny hand, checking the readouts on the stand next to the cot.

"She's stable." For the moment, although he knew that could change at any time. "She'll be watched carefully, but I can leave a call number for us at the desk if it'll make you feel better."

"Yes. It would. Thank you."

Dean wasn't sure why she wanted them to ring her rather than the baby's own mother, but he knew better than to ask.

Snapping off his gloves and discarding them, he motioned toward the door. "I'll just go hang up my coat and sign out. Do you want to meet me by the front door of the maternity unit?"

She nodded. "I'll let my sister know where I'm going." Without another word, she slid through the door of the SCBU and headed down the hallway, her red dress swishing around her hips in a way that made him rethink just how tired he was.

Too tired.

And she worked at the hospital.

A combination that had "do not touch" written all over it.

Dean had never been one to play by any set of rules except his own. But this was definitely one of them: don't get involved with any one female…and especially not one he worked with on a regular basis. Even though Jess didn't work on his floor and he didn't see her every day, it still counted. Getting too involved could get tricky. And ugly.

If ever he needed to stick to the game plan, it was now. He'd been able to abide by his inner rules in the past. And he could damn well do it now.

* * *

Jess recognized the place. All those rumors about Dean were usually centered around this particular restaurant—as in he'd been spotted here. More than once, and always with a woman in tow.

She swallowed. With soft lighting and half walls that divided the space into smaller clusters of diners, she could see why. The restaurant fostered an atmosphere of quiet intimacy.

For what? Discreet affairs?

Jess wasn't sure what madness had her sitting across from the playboy of Cambridge Royal, but something had obviously addled her brain. And from the way the hostess greeted him by name, eyes journeying over his tie and dress shirt—and the way he filled it out—as they came through the door, he'd been here many times before.

That brought up another question. The tie. Where had he come up with that? Did he keep one in his office just for spur-of-the-moment dinner dates? If so, it evidently got a lot of use. It would seem those rumors were true.

Which brought her back around to the insanity of being here. With him.

That argument with her sister and its aftermath had left her heartsick. Even her mum had shot her a couple of disappointed glances as they'd waited for the doctors to check Abbie over.

Had she done enough to avoid that confrontation? She'd tried to shut it down, but, in her desperation to get away, she'd been much harsher than necessary.

But the idea that she'd been engaging in some long-distance pillow talk with Martin while he was away on business trips was so ludicrous, she hadn't been sure how to answer her. Abbie didn't even have proof that Martin was engaging in anything of the sort. With anyone.

Just some vague messages on his phone that could have meant anything.

Why hadn't Jess just walked away the second she realized her sister's temper was beginning to flare out of control? Instead, she'd stood there and defended herself in front of a roomful of guests. Moving the venue of the anniversary party to Cambridge had already made for a tense atmosphere, and by fighting with Abbie in the middle of their celebration she'd made things worse for everyone. Including that little one hooked up to machines in the Special Care Unit.

God. Her eyes closed as another shard of guilt stabbed through her stomach.

"Hey. You okay?"

Dean's voice had a gruff soothing quality as it drifted over her. One she'd never noticed before this second.

She blinked back to awareness. Exactly what did that mean? She only crossed paths with the man in those odd moments when their jobs intersected, which wasn't all that often. Her midwife duties kept her in one section of the hospital, while Dean's kept him in another.

But you noticed him. You know you did. How could you not with all that gossip about his exploits?

Yes. She'd heard those stories. Time and time again. Only no one she knew had actually claimed to have made it into Dean Edwards' bed. Or anywhere else, for that matter. But he'd been seen around Cambridge. And never with the same woman. The descriptions varied, but the pattern didn't.

"I'm fine." She toyed with her serviette. It was on the tip of her tongue to ask for the fifth time if he was sure it was all right to leave the baby, but she clamped down on it just in time to stop the question from emerging. The hospital would ring if there was any change.

The waiter arrived with a bottle and a question on his face. When Dean nodded, the man poured white wine into both of their glasses. Not that she needed to be drinking at a time like this. But it was only one glass, and, since she didn't keep any kind of alcohol in her house because of her dad, she didn't get to indulge all that often. Maybe it would stop the mad pounding in her chest at sitting across from the first attractive man in...well, since she and Martin had broken it off. Her sister might as well have poisoned the entire male species. Or at least made Jess feel like the consolation prize to anyone who might show some interest. Because when she was set side by side with her sister, Abbie was the one they'd chosen. Every. Single. Time.

She and Abbie might look alike, but their personalities were at opposite ends of the spectrum. Jess was the socially awkward one, the one who had trouble forming and keeping deep friendships, while Abbie was vivacious and outgoing, able to charm anyone she came in contact with. And her sister always got what she wanted.

And what she'd wanted was the very thing Jess had always dreamed of having. A place where she lived in no one else's shadow...where she truly belonged. At one time she'd equated that with having her own home and family.

When that possibility had been ripped away, she'd thrown herself into her job, doing all she could for her patients and their little ones. Maybe her parents were right. Maybe she was too dedicated. Looking at her tiny new niece had made her stomach churn with a longing she'd all but forgotten.

This was Abbie's fourth baby.

Jess had none. And no prospects of a serious relationship or any children in the near future.

She picked up her glass of wine, swirling the liquid to block the direction of her thoughts. Conversation. That was what she needed. Racking her brain, she tried to think of something that would break the growing silence. Something witty. Something that would make her feel a little less dull. Dean's eyes were now on her, a slight furrow forming between his brows.

Say something!

"I've never been here before. Do you come here often?"

Oh, no! Why had she asked that, of all things? A few seconds of silence followed the question before he spoke.

"Often enough."

His jaw tightened a fraction.

This was definitely where he brought his women.

His women?

She crinkled her nose at that thought. Wow, she was really outdoing herself tonight. Worse, what if someone she knew was here? She sank a little lower in her seat, taking a sip of wine and swallowing it. "Really? It's my very first time."

Dean, who'd been in the process of lifting his glass to his lips, stopped with it midway to its goal. The furrow between his brows deepened, then he gave his head a slight shake as if clearing it and took a drink. A good-sized one if the movement of his throat was any indication.

Did he think she was flirting with him? She hoped not, because if he did, there was no telling what he might—

"What are you thinking about?"

Caught!

"My niece."

Those words brought her back to earth with a bump. Her niece's situation was the only reason she was sitting here in this restaurant.

Could the newborn sense the antagonism flowing between her and her sister, even in the SCBU? Abbie hadn't spoken to her since the baby's delivery, despite her mother's attempts at playing peacemaker.

Poor Mum. Some anniversary this had turned out to be.

He set his wine down. "You said it was your fault. You know that's not true."

"Abbie and I were in the middle of a row. She went into labor. If I'd just walked away…"

Would the outcome have been any different? Abbie had been bound and determined to have her say.

But surely Jess could have changed the direction of the conversation. Maybe. Her sister had always known exactly which buttons to push—which insecurities to choose—to get her going. Today had been no exception.

"Coincidence."

"Really? Stress can induce labor—you know that as well as I do." She paused a beat and then let the rest of it out. "She thought I was sending suggestive texts to her husband."

That got a reaction. Dean's eyes narrowed just a touch. "Were you?"

"No!" She fiddled again with the corner of her serviette. "I mean, Martin and I were engaged at one time, but once he saw Abbie—"

She couldn't finish the sentence.

Instead of pressing her for details, Dean chuckled.

That shocked her. "I don't see what's so funny."

"Well, not funny exactly. So your sister had her eye on your fiancé, and now that she has his ring on her finger, she's worried you might want him back."

That was it in a nutshell. It had been six years, but Abbie just couldn't let it go. It was one of the reasons Jess had moved to Cambridge in the first place, to get away from the constant haranguing and jealous questioning.

"I don't want him. At all."

"I can well imagine."

Which brought her back to the current dilemma. "I have no idea how to make her believe me."

The conversation paused when the waiter brought their food. Curried chicken with rice and vegetables served family style. Before she could lift a finger, Dean had taken her plate and dished up some of the fragrant food. Too bad she didn't have much of an appetite at the moment.

Once Dean had served himself, he had no problem picking up where they'd left off. "So you think your sister is going to keep accusing you of trying to steal her husband...aka your ex."

Using her fork, she speared a piece of chicken. "She lives in London, so, once she goes back, I'm hoping it'll die back down. Or that Martin will be able to convince her we're not communicating behind her back."

"Mmm...I see." He popped a bite into his mouth and chewed. Swallowed.

Why was she even telling him any of this? And what was with her watching the man's throat? It had to be the way that sharp edge of his Adam's apple dipped, causing her eyes to want to follow it. All the way down to his... She jerked her eyes back to his face.

Dean continued. "No current love interest to throw her off the trail?"

"No." She hurriedly stuffed a piece of food into her mouth, even as she felt her face heat all over again. If he only knew how true those words were, he would think she was a complete washout when it came to the opposite sex.

In fact, the two of them should not even be having this conversation. She barely knew the man.

But what she did know of him... He was rumored to have a revolving bedroom door. Women in...women out. Swish, swish, swish turned that door.

"What if you did?" he murmured.

"Excuse me?"

He smiled at that. "You're not going to turn that cute little glare back on, are you?"

"Excuse…I mean, what?"

"That's better." He set his fork down and reached across to touch his fingers to hers. A shot of electricity arced through her hand and zipped straight up her arm. "I was just sitting here thinking. Maybe you should hand her proof of a conquest or two?"

It was said with a cheeky air that made her laugh. Not because it was funny, but because he said it as though it weren't such a stretch to imagine that she might have a long list of failed romances.

She didn't. She left things like that to her sister. And to men like Dean.

"I don't have any conquests."

His index finger brushed along hers, sending another shiver through her. "Do you always say exactly what you think, Jessica Black?"

"No." Although that wasn't quite right. She did tend to wear her heart on her sleeve, which was why her sister had always been able to zero in on what Jess wanted out of life—on which boy Jess liked. Then she turned on her million-kilowatt charm and took it for herself.

"Oh, I think you do." The low words curled around her midriff, squeezing the air from her lungs. "But maybe we can use that to our advantage."

"Um…we?"

"Mmm." He leaned across the table. "How about if we show your sister exactly how her little game is played."

"I—I have no idea what you're talking about."

"I think you need to show her you can round up your own men, thank you very much."

"Men? Plural?"

"Why not?"

Her gut churned. "How can you do that?"

"Do what?"

"Go to bed with hundreds of women as if it's nothing special."

His gaze hardened. "The hospital grapevine strikes again."

"It's not like you haven't been seen here. You have. The hostess knows your name, for heaven's sake." The words just kept pouring out. "I'm not judging. I just don't know how it's possible to have casual sex without feeling something...anything. Do the women just go along with it? Or do you simply stop ringing them after you've gotten what you wanted?"

The bitterness of everything that had happened with Martin came rushing back. The giving of her heart—her body—and then having him stop ringing her one day. Finding out he'd been seen with her sister and to have them show up at her door and spill the beans, that he'd been going out with Abbie while still engaged to her.

"What makes you think that the 'casual' in casual sex isn't on both sides? That the woman isn't just as interested in keeping things simple? Have you ever tried it?"

"Well, no." And she hadn't. Maybe that was why it seemed impossible to believe that two people could share a bed and then each go their separate ways the next day with no hurt feelings—no misunderstandings.

"Maybe you should. It's a hell of a lot different when neither party expects anything out of the arrangement other than a single night of pleasure."

The way his gravelly voice touched that last word sent a ripple through her midsection. What would it be like to have your physical needs met and then not expect anything further?

Maybe he was right. Maybe it wasn't as bad as it sounded.

And it could make her sister finally believe she was over Martin…that she'd been over him for a long time.

"Maybe I should."

One side of his mouth went up, and he leaned over the table. "Bet you can't."

She sat up a little straighter. If he could do it, surely she could. Unless he was calling her a prude. "Of course I can."

"Prove it."

Oh, no. This was not where she'd seen this conversation heading. "And how exactly am I supposed to do that? Are you going to hide in a cupboard and watch me?"

"No." A little of the mellowness in his voice had faded and a sharper edge had appeared. "But I can feel out the men. Make sure they're safe."

Jess could not believe she was even having this conversation. "So you would interview any prospective bed mate to make sure they aren't a serial rapist? Exactly where would this 'finding my own men' be done? A pub?"

One thing Jess was good at was sizing up personalities. Except how good had she been at sizing up Martin? Not great. Maybe she did need someone to help scope things out. Not that she was actually thinking of doing anything of the sort.

Was she?

Evidently she was.

"A pub is perfect," he said.

He didn't say it, but she got the distinct impression that that was where Dean picked up some of his prospective one-night stands.

Suddenly Jess was backpedaling like mad. She really didn't think she could go through with it, but, since she'd criticized Dean, she could understand why he'd taken offense. Just because *she* didn't have casual sex once a week didn't make it wrong that he did. "And you would be what? My wingman?"

He tossed his serviette on the table. "Your wingman." He said it as if sounding it out. "I like it. I think that would work."

Oh, no, she had no intention of doing anything like what Dean was proposing. But the thought of letting the man see how much it bothered her...

What if she made it look as if she were going along with it? That way, even if she wiggled her way out of the dates, she could still tell her sister she was going out. Maybe it would even ease some of the bad feelings between them.

A thought came to her. What if Dean picked up a woman while she was there? The last thing she wanted was to see him walk out of that pub with someone. She had no idea why, but she didn't. "So let's say I agree to chat up three men—" she was careful not to actually say she would go on to have sex with these men "—then you have to do something as well. How about, you have to promise to leave the pub alone. Go without. See how the other side lives."

"So basically you would be the only one having fun?"

"Exactly. Think you can handle it?"

Dean leaned forward, one brow raised at the challenge. "Sweetheart, you've got yourself a bet."

CHAPTER THREE

DEAN HAD NO idea why he'd goaded Jess into that ridiculous bet. They'd gone to the pub twice so far and she'd easily found herself a partner both nights, slipping out of the place within an hour.

He wasn't sure why he'd done it. Or why he'd been so adamant about going with her. Maybe because it bothered him that she compared herself to her sister. And she did. He heard it in her words, saw it in the uncertain way her fingers twisted together when she talked about her.

And his own part of the bet?

Laughable, because she seemed to think he picked up a different woman every night.

It would be kind of hard to do his job if he spent all his nights having wild sex. Although he could think of one woman he might be tempted to make that sacrifice for.

Not that he would.

Especially since he'd promised that very woman that he would have no sex. At all. At least not for the next several nights.

"Dr. Edwards? Is everything all right?"

Sitting in a rocking chair in the corner and holding a tiny baby to his shoulder, he realized he'd zoned out for a few seconds. "Fine. I'm just getting ready to put her back."

His job didn't necessarily include cuddling his charges,

but there was something about this one. Born to a drug-addicted mum, the little boy was off to a rocky start. But at least the child-welfare people had stepped in and insisted the mother clean up her act before allowing her anywhere near the child.

That was more than he had gotten when he was young. Then again, it was his father who'd had the addiction problem, not his mother.

He rubbed a few more gentle circles across the newborn's back. At least the baby had quieted down. When pregnant women took drugs, there were two victims. The baby's mother...and her child, who was now suffering through withdrawals—through no fault of his own.

Standing to his feet, he gave the nurse a quick smile before tucking the baby back into his cot. "Feel free to page me if this happens again."

She nodded, smiling back.

Young and attractive with curly brown hair and sparkling eyes, Deidre had made it a point to call him back whenever she had a particularly difficult case. He wondered if that was for the baby's benefit or hers. It didn't matter. He'd decided a long time ago it was better to leave his personal life at home and his professional life at the hospital. It was just better that way.

"You have such a way with them."

Did he? It seemed that anyone who offered these little guys a bit of love and affection would get the same response. And maybe that stemmed back to his childhood as well. He didn't want any of them to feel as alone as he'd once felt. And this particular baby had quieted down almost as soon as he'd settled into the rocker with him.

"I think it's just the body contact."

She raised her brows and went over to look at the

now sleeping infant. "No, I think you just have the magic touch."

Not so magic.

He glanced at his watch, his jaw tightening. Tonight was the last night of his and Jess's bet, and suddenly the last thing he wanted to do was watch her walk out of that pub with yet another man. He'd made her ring him at home as soon as she arrived, and again after the man left her house, so that he would know she was safe.

Another thing he was nonplussed about. Of course she was safe. Jess was a grown woman and between the two of them they'd picked out the meekest, mildest-looking men they could.

Okay, that was probably all him, because Jess had talked to a couple of attractive muscular-looking chaps, but they'd made him uneasy.

Or was it just that he couldn't stand the idea of her spending the night with someone she might actually decide to go out with more than once.

Nope. That wasn't it at all. And just to prove it, tonight, he would let Jess pick out whoever she wanted.

And he wouldn't do a thing to stop her.

Having a wingman was the pits.

On their third and final outing, Jess was glad it was their last. Her days were spent with her niece, and her nights…well, her nights were Dean's. But not in the traditional sense.

As much as she wanted to skip out of the pub and go home alone, Dean was always there. Always checking out the patrons. And, hell, if he didn't always steer her toward men that looked as if they were laced tighter than a corset. It was never the good-looking ladies' man, or anyone who was like Dean himself. No. In fact, whenever one of those types hit on her, somehow Dean was always there with a glare or a sharp word.

Why did he even care? Wasn't this all about the bet—about seeing what it was like to have a few nights of casual sex? That was what it had started out as.

Instead, Dean brooded. Off in the corner, he would nurse a glass of Scotch and watch her sit awkwardly at the bar. If he approved of whoever offered to buy her a drink he stayed put, if he didn't...well, if he didn't, he appeared next to her like an avenging angel and chased the man off.

So for the last two date nights—Jess had faked it. She pretended to leave with one of the pre-approved men and then bolted, feigning a headache or stomach virus. Maybe it was fortunate that the men were as nervous and unsure as she was, because it meant she went home alone.

Her one consolation was that Dean left by himself as well. At least, if he was keeping to his side of the bargain. From his grouchy demeanor at the hospital over the last couple of days, she'd say he really had slept alone.

Why that mattered, she had no idea.

She screwed up her courage for one last run, and went over to the bar, asking for a dark bitter ale—which she hated. Her friend Amy promised Jess would eventually get used to the stuff if she drank it often enough. Right now, she just wasn't seeing it. But it was cheap and Amy swore men were impressed by a woman who drank dark ale. Hmm. Her friend was single and pregnant, so while it might attract them, that was evidently all it did. Which might work in Jess's favor, actually.

She should probably give Amy a call and make sure everything was going okay.

Thank God this was the last night. Even Abbie and her parents had seemed surprised when she told them she had plans again this evening.

"Another date?" The hope in her mum's voice would have been comical had it not been so very far from reality.

She'd mumbled something that she hoped made sense and then slunk from the room and away from Abbie's suspicious eyes.

Sighing, she perched on the nearest stool and forced a sip down, glancing across the space and meeting Dean's eye. This evening he was in a snug black T-shirt and faded jeans, the combination doing a number on her tummy. She'd never seen him dressed this informally. He lifted his own drink—something that looked a whole lot stronger than hers—and gave her a mocking salute before taking a swig of it.

Why was he even here? Surely not to make sure she did what she promised. Because he didn't look particularly happy to be sitting there waiting for her to leave with her next victim. Or maybe he was just irritated that he wasn't going to take someone home himself. Either way, this wasn't fun anymore. Not that it ever had been.

Someone tapped her shoulder, and Jess turned her barstool to meet the smile of a blue-eyed ginger. "You're a fan of ale, I see."

The Scottish burr gave away his nationality, rolling across her in a way that made her smile right back. "Not actually, but I'm trying to learn."

The man leaned forward and gave an audible sniff. "Dark Lady. Not a bad choice."

Okay, so maybe Amy was on to something. "Are you a fan?"

"I am now." Jess wasn't sure if he was talking about the ale or about her. She sized him up. Just how hard was he going to be to get rid of when it came time to leave?

When he covered her hand with his, she had her

answer. She tensed, a trickle of panic beginning to gather in her midsection.

She didn't want to make anyone angrier than neces- sary. Especially a man like this one. She got the feeling he might be a little more difficult to shake.

Swallowing, she wondered if she could glance back at Dean and get his attention. They hadn't set up a signal in case she got in over her head. So maybe she should...

The back of her neck prickled just as her newfound companion's brows pulled together. His hand tightened over hers.

"I was wondering where you'd gotten off to, Jess."

Dean.

Had he read her mind? As much as she'd been think- ing about sending out an SOS, what she really wanted to do was leave and get this whole bet thing over with. It had been beyond stupid. A time waster. For both of them. She never would be a casual-sex type of girl, no matter how hard he tried to convince her otherwise. It was all fun and games...until someone lost an eye—or their heart.

Not that she was in danger of that from this particular ale aficionado.

But from Dean?

Lord, she hoped not.

She spun around, suddenly deciding she didn't want or need his help. He'd decided he didn't approve of this par- ticular man? Well, she would show him that, from now on, *she* made those kinds of decisions.

Up went her brows. She needed to cut him off before he got started. The last couple of times he'd wanted to get rid of a man who had his eye on her, he'd pretended to be her significant other.

"Mum isn't expecting us home until later." She smirked up at him, daring him to contradict her.

His response? A slow, knowing smile.

"Mum knows what we're like, when we're out on the town." He took the ale from her hand and set it in front of the Scotsman. "Enjoy."

The man let go of her, his possessiveness appearing to change to horror when Dean lifted a brow and said, "Dance with me…sis."

Then he whirled her into his arms and headed toward the floor where other couples were already moving to the beat of some slow song.

Jess couldn't hold back a laugh. "I can't believe you just did that. You've probably scarred that man for life."

There was no way she was going to admit she was relieved. Relieved she wasn't going to have to try to wave him off on her own.

"I can't believe you called me your brother."

"Serves you right for interfering."

He leaned back to study her face. "Did you want to leave with him?"

No, she didn't want to leave with him or anyone. But she'd gotten herself into a mess and wasn't sure how to get herself back out of it. "I thought we had a deal. I leave with three different men, and you leave with no one."

"I've changed my mind."

A warning tingle began at the back of her skull. "What do you mean you've changed your mind? Are you reneging on the bet?"

"Yes." The word brushed across her, and the tingle became a full-fledged shiver.

He pressed his cheek to hers and drew her closer. If the Scotsman wasn't scarred before at the way Dean had whisked her away, he probably was now.

Jess swallowed. "I'm not sure what you mean."

"I mean neither of us is leaving with a stranger. Not you.

Not me." His hand tightened on hers just the way the Scotsman's had. The intimate contact filled her with alarm, but a completely different kind of alarm. Because she liked it.

"Well, you not leaving with someone was kind of the point, wasn't it?" Although her voice sounded as shaky as her legs felt, she managed a smile.

"I'm forfeiting. As of now."

So he *was* tired of frittering his nights away with nothing to show for it in the end. She should be glad. Because that meant she didn't have to pretend to leave with anyone now.

But she wasn't glad. And she wasn't quite sure why. "You're a free man. I assume you already have someone in mind."

"I do."

Jess turned her head, trying to figure out who the lucky woman was.

He tucked his fingers under her chin and shifted her face back toward his. "You're wrong. Are you so oblivious about what you do to a man like that?" He nodded in the direction of the bar where she'd sat a few moments ago.

"I'm not sure what you mean."

"He wanted to take you home with him."

"Oh." Of course she knew that, but then again people in places like this probably weren't particularly choosy. After all, they were here for the same reason that Dean probably came here. To find a companion for a night of sex.

He chuckled. "You really don't have any idea, do you?" His fingers left her chin and trailed up the line of her jaw. "There's only one woman I'm interested in leaving with."

"Who?" The trembling in her legs came back full force.

"Let's just say I'm thinking some *very* unbrotherly thoughts right now."

Her? He wanted to leave with her. Why?

Wasn't it obvious? Casual sex, remember?

It was on the tip of her tongue to give him a resounding yes and leap into his arms. But whatever had been niggling in the back of her head grew as she thought through the implications. He was tired of playing the wingman...tired of his little hunger strike. And now he was hoping to break his fast. What easier target than the person he'd coaxed into taking this ridiculous bet in the first place? The person he'd dared to have casual sex with three different men. How easy would it be for Dean to be that third man?

It had nothing to do with her at all. She could be a plastic mannequin for all he cared.

Casual sex, indeed. Maybe that was good enough for him, but it wasn't for her. He might think her a prude, but she didn't care anymore.

Hurt surged up from somewhere inside her—a large festering lump that threatened to burst open in front of everyone in the pub.

"I don't think so, Dean. I have no clue what put this idea into your head, but you can put it right back out. If you want someone to pass the night with, you'd better keep on looking. Because this girl is leaving this whole scene. Alone."

With that, Jess yanked free of Dean's hold and stomped out of the pub and into the night.

CHAPTER FOUR

THE BABY WASN'T BREATHING.

The second the newborn was placed in his hands, Dean went into full crisis mode, belting out orders, even as he raced through possible treatment options, ruling them out one by one. Exhaustion pulled at his limbs, but at least he was able to put that fiasco with Jess last night out of his head. For now. He had no space for anything but what was currently happening in this room.

The victim of a drunk driver, the newborn's mother had been fatally struck as she crossed an intersection to go to work. CPR at the scene and efforts to resuscitate at Cambridge Royal had proved unsuccessful. The decision was made to put mum on life support and do an emergency C-section in an effort to save the baby, even as a grief-stricken husband waited outside the surgical suite.

"Let's bag her." He laid the baby on a table and a manual resuscitator was placed in his hand.

"Come on, sweetheart." The words whispered through his skull, with each squeeze of the Ambu bag. The tiny chest rose and fell. There was a heartbeat, but, so far, no effort at breathing on her own.

Going through his mental checklist, he had one of the nurses take over the bagging so he could test reflexes. He was gratified to see there were at least some reactions, though not what he would have liked. But babies' brains weren't fully developed. He'd seen some amazing recoveries in newborns even more premature than this one.

Most had not been deprived of oxygen for this long, however.

He glanced at his watch. Five minutes since delivery.

"Stop pushing air for a moment and let's see what we've got."

The nurse lifted the BVM and the whole world stopped breathing. At least Dean did. Then there was a gasp. And the kick of a small leg.

Suddenly the baby's face screwed up tight, and she let out a squeaked puff of air. Her lungs reinflated, and it became a full-fledged cry. Joined by another. Then another.

The sense of relief couldn't have been greater if it had been Dean's own flesh and blood lying on that metal table. Because at least the new father wouldn't have to mourn two deaths. And the baby's mum, still on a ventilator behind them, might be able to save more lives through organ donation, which was what her husband said she would have wanted.

"Let's take her down to Special Care to do the rest of the workup." The sooner they got her into one of the incubators, the better for her tiny lungs. They would monitor her for a while to make sure she kept breathing and remained stable.

The second they arrived on the ward, Dean noticed Jess's sister was in the room, seated beside her baby's incubator, but she didn't have exam gloves on. Nor did she have her hands through the openings so she could touch her baby's skin. Instead, she just sat there slumped forward. Glancing at the observation window behind him, he spied Jess. Her face was turned away as if she were staring at something down the hall. Maybe she just couldn't face looking at her sister.

He hadn't spoken with Jess since that disastrous scene last night at the pub. Why the hell had he pulled something like that?

He had no idea.

Turning his attention back to his newest charge, he directed the staff as they hooked the newborn up to the monitors and checked the baby's oxygen levels. So far, things were looking more hopeful than they had for the last half-hour.

"Let me know if anything changes."

Satisfied that everything was under control with this particular baby, he headed over to where Jess's sister sat and greeted her. When he asked if she wanted to interact with the baby she shook her head. "I don't want to do anything that would hurt her."

Something in her face tightened, and her eyes strayed toward the window.

Ahhh...so she did know her sister was there. When he turned his attention in that direction, he noted that Jess was now looking at both of them. And something in her stricken expression made his chest ache. Surely they could put what had happened between them last night aside—for a little while, at least. He motioned her inside. Jess hesitated, and he wondered if she might ignore him for a second, but, finally, she pushed through the door and slowly headed their way.

"I don't want her here." The low, angry words made him blink. The ache in his chest tightened even further.

These two women might look alike, but he'd been right earlier. The resemblance began and ended there.

"She's your baby's aunt," he said.

"And she caused this." Her hand swept around the room. "All of it."

"She caused *all* of these babies' problems?" He knew what she meant, but he wanted to hear her actually say the words. To say that she blamed Jess for what happened.

The woman's head jerked as she looked up at him. "Of course not. But my baby is here because of her."

When he realized Jess was close enough to have heard the ugly words, his heart hardened into a rock. The same rock he'd carried as a child when his father's anger had come at him and his mum in the form of ridicule or through his fists. But when Jess made to turn around and flee, he reached out and caught her by the wrist before addressing Abbie again. "No. Your baby is here because she was born too early. Nothing more. Nothing less."

The nurses working on the other baby threw them a curious glance, but he didn't budge. Jess had worried herself sick over her niece as evidenced by her vigil over the incubator that first night. And the way she made sure the nursing staff had her mobile number and made them promise to ring her at the first hint of trouble.

It took repeated tugging before he got her close enough to slide his arm behind her back and hold her in place, and even then she looked as if she wanted to crawl under the nearest rock. Or the nearest incubator. But he was not going to let her run away the way he'd once done. She was going to stand and face this particular bully head-on. And unlike Dean when he was a child, she would not have to do that alone.

Right on cue, Abbie's glance cut from one to the other before settling on the point of contact between the two of them. "Exactly what is going on here?"

Beneath his hand, Jess squirmed, and he was quite sure she wanted to ask him what the hell he thought he was doing. But she didn't. Nor had she made the slightest effort to defend herself in the face of her sister's ire.

Something swelled up inside of him—an urge to protect that was both familiar and foreign. Time to put someone firmly in her place. And he thought he knew the perfect way to do that. He was pretty sure Jess was going to kill him later, but he'd deal with that fallout when the time came.

He allowed his arm to drop, and when he glanced at her face, it was pink. Very pink. And it looked good on her.

One of the nurses came over to tell him the baby he'd worked on was settled in and seemed stable. "Good, thank you. I'll keep an eye on her for a while."

With that, the pair left the room, leaving just Dean, Jess and her sister.

Abbie again addressed them. "Does someone want to tell me what's going on?"

Here went nothing.

"I take it Jess didn't tell you?"

Two pairs of brown eyes swung to look at him.

"Tell me what?"

He draped his arm back around her shoulders. "Don't be shy, sweetheart. Tell her."

Jess's mouth popped open, eyes widening in horror. "What?"

"I'm sure they've wondered where you've been the last couple of nights."

"Dean…" The warning in her voice was unmistakable. But he'd come too far to turn back now.

"Jess and I have been going out." It wasn't exactly a lie. They had been going out to the pub, after all. Her sister didn't need to know that Jess had turned him down flat as far as anything else went.

"Going out. You expect me to believe that?"

Anger pumped through his veins at the open disbelief in Abbie's voice. Suddenly, he was very sure he was doing the right thing.

And if this little farce got out? Well, worse things had been said about him—at least from what he'd heard here and there.

Leaning down to her ear, he whispered, "I'll explain later. Just play along."

Out loud, he said, "It's recent. We're keeping it quiet. For now." Another half-truth. Their going out had been recent. And he was pretty sure Jess wanted it kept quiet.

Jess didn't agree. Or disagree. But a little of the sneer left her sister's face.

"So what you said at the party… All of those texts Martin got wasn't about you trying—"

Jess finally found her voice. "I've told you that. Many times, Abbie. Martin and I have been over for a long, long time. He loves you. Not me."

So it was true. Jess had once been engaged to Abbie's husband. And Abbie thought her sister still had the hots for him.

He looked at her with new eyes. If he had to choose between the sisters right here right now, there would be no question as to who he'd go with.

Jess. Hands down.

"I guess I owe you both an apology, then."

"No, you—"

Dean squeezed her shoulder to stop the words. Abbie did owe her an apology, from what he'd seen. A big one.

"But as for the baby…" The woman's glance went back to her child. She leaned forward a little. "What's that on her leg?" She pointed at the incubator and tapped the side of it. The newborn startled for a second, then relaxed.

"What?" Jess shook off his hand and moved closer.

"There. That red thing on her calf."

There was a small red mark the size of a thumbprint on the side of the baby's leg.

The relief on Jess's face was almost comical. "It's just a little birthmark. A port wine stain. It's nothing."

"A port what?" Abbie trailed her fingers over the Plexiglas side as if tracing the mark. "Will it go away?"

"Probably not, but it's nothing serious. I promise."

There was a pause before Abbie spoke again. "I don't want people to make fun of her."

There was a note of sadness—or maybe it was fear—in her voice. It made Dean take a closer look, seeing something of himself in her words. Had Abbie been made fun of at some point by someone? It would explain some of that angry defensiveness she seemed to carry around with her. He'd had a little of that himself when he'd been younger. More so after his dad went to prison and his mum took off for parts unknown when he was just sixteen.

Dean had been angry all right. Angry at his parents. Angry at the group home he'd been placed in. Angry at life in general. Until he'd learned to harness that anger and put it to good use. And that included not pinning his hopes on any one human being. At some point, they all let you down.

"I'm sure they won't," Jess said. "Why would they?"

Her sister sniffed as if she was not about to listen to anything Jess had to say. Then she stood. "I think I'll go back to my room. I'm knackered."

She'd still made no move to touch her baby, and that bothered Dean more than he wanted to admit. Everyone had his or her own way of dealing with emotional pain, but to shut off physical contact with her own child?

Well, hadn't he wished from time to time that his father had cut off physical contact? But he hadn't. It had taken

putting Dean's mum in hospital that last time to keep the
man from hurting them again.

"Do you want someone to walk you back to your
room?" he asked.

Abbie shook her head. "I can manage. You'll ring me
if there's any change?"

Dean might have thought the words were meant for
Jess, except she was looking directly at him. Ignoring her
sister just as she was ignoring her baby. "Someone will.
Yes." He was not going to let her use him to wound Jess
even more.

She left the room without so much as a thank you or
another glance at her child.

The second she was gone, Jess dropped into the seat
her sister had just vacated. "Oh, my God, why on earth
did you do that?"

He wasn't sure why, himself. Maybe the urge to protect was overdeveloped in him—the result of having no
one to defend him as a child. That could also explain why
he'd felt such a strong need to help the most vulnerable of
humans: newborns in crisis.

"Well, it wasn't a total fabrication. We do have The
Pub." He said it as if it were some special shared memory,
rather than a total washout.

She actually smiled. "Did you have any luck after I
left?"

Dean hadn't stuck around. He'd followed her…staying
far enough behind for her not to notice, but close enough
to know she made it to her car without that big Scot fol-
lowing her.

"I decided to stick to the rules, after all."

"Oh." She blinked a couple of times as if surprised.
"Well, anyway, thanks for what you did a few minutes
ago. It wasn't necessary, though. It didn't seem to matter

to her one way or the other, except maybe she finally believes I'm not after her husband."

"Oh, it mattered. She just wasn't going to let you see it."

If anyone knew, he did. How many times had he hidden his feelings from his father? Dean had stood there and let the man do his worst without crying or pleading for him to stop. Because he'd learned to detach himself from what was happening to and around him. As a result, he'd learned to keep his emotions tucked away to the point of *almost* denying he had any.

Except when he did foolhardy stuff like pretending to be someone's significant other for no good reason. And it had been foolhardy. Because dancing with her at the pub, getting to know the way her eyes crinkled when she laughed affected him on a level he hadn't known existed. Maybe because he'd never bothered to truly get to know the women he dated.

Like that thin streak of gray he'd noticed over the past couple of nights when she'd tucked her hair behind her ears. It almost blended in with the rest of the blonde strands, but not quite.

"Where did you get this?" He couldn't resist touching the silky lock now.

"The gray, you mean?" Her smile widened. "A llama at a petting zoo decided to get a little too friendly with my hair clip when I was a kid. It yanked the clip—and a good hunk of my hair—out and chewed on them for a while before deciding they weren't so great, after all. When the hair grew back, it was white."

He ran the bleached-out tresses between his fingers. "Your sister doesn't have this, then."

"No, she doesn't." She gave a slight shrug. "It's my own personal souvenir."

A visible reminder of past hurt. Thankfully his own

past remained invisible to the world, even if the after-math still bubbled up inside of him from time to time. It was one reason he hadn't wanted to work with toddlers or young children. His suspicious mind would probably jump to conclusions each time a boy or girl presented with a broken arm. Or a broken heart.

No. This was where he belonged.

Jess leaned forward and glanced at her niece, the act tugging her hair from his fingers. "I never even noticed the spot on her leg before," she murmured.

"Because it's not important."

"It is to Abbie."

His fingers itched to give her hand a reassuring squeeze. He curled them into a ball at his side, instead. "It may fade with time."

"My sister has always tried so hard to be perfect. She's incredibly disciplined about everything she does."

"And you're not?"

She shrugged. "I don't expect everyone around me to live up to a certain set of expectations."

"You expect yourself to live up to them, instead."

She paused. "Maybe." She glanced up at him. "Can I hold her?"

Dean nodded. "Of course. Only for a minute or two, though."

It took a little doing to manage all the tubes and wires, but the second the baby was placed in her arms, Jess was in love. From her little pink cap to the teeny-tiny nappy, Marissa Fay Stewart was as perfect as could be. She didn't stir other than to twitch a shoulder as she set-tled into place.

Jess cuddled her with one arm while she stroked a gloved thumb down the newborn's leg. She didn't understand why Abbie didn't want to stay by her cot. Why she didn't seem to even want to hold her baby. Was she just afraid?

Her sister was a good mother to her other three children. At least from what she'd heard from her parents— the kids were all happy and well-adjusted. Maybe that was it. It had to be a huge adjustment to add another child to their family. Her sister would come around.

She touched the little mark on her calf, just barely visible from where she sat. "She's gorgeous."

"She is." Dean agreed with her without hesitation. When she glanced up at him, though, his eyes weren't on the baby. They were on her.

Her face heated and she ducked her head again, hoping he didn't notice the way he affected her. This was why almost every female in the hospital swooned over him, including some of the babies' mums.

Well, Jess wasn't about to be one of those women. Not even a pretend one. If what he'd said was true, that her sister believed his little charade, then they were going to leave it at that. No need to take it any further.

The sound of something tapping on the viewing glass across the room caught her attention and things went from bad to worse. Martin stood there waving at her. Why wasn't he with his wife?

She clenched her teeth at her own stupidity. Maybe he'd already been to Abbie's room. He must have ended his business trip early when he heard the news.

Dean gave her a questioning look.

"It's the baby's father. Martin."

"The same Martin who left you for your sister."

She cringed, but it was true. Hearing it said out loud though brought back a whole host of awful memories. But

Dean was no longer beside her, he was striding toward the door, letting in her ex…her sister's husband.

"I was in Tokyo, and had a dickens of a time finding a flight out. How is she, Abbie?"

Jess froze at the mistake. Before she could say anything, though, Dean moved beside her. "Look again."

Her ex glanced at her. "Oh, hell, sorry, Jess. You were holding the baby, and I just assumed…"

"It's okay. Abbie's tired. She's in her room. I take it you haven't been to see her yet?"

"I thought I'd find her here, actually." He squatted down beside her chair. "Is the baby okay?"

The tears that hadn't come earlier now stung her eyes. "She's tiny. But perfect."

"And Abbie? Is she all right?"

"Yes. She's upset, naturally, but she's doing well physically." She decided to leave out the details of what had transpired, pretty sure someone would soon enlighten him as to her part in the ordeal.

He touched the baby's head. "She looks like you two."

A hand came to rest on her shoulder, and Jess stiffened when she realized it was Dean. A trill of apprehension went through her, and, as much as the rational part of her brain was yelling at her to shake off his touch, she just sat there without a word.

Martin noticed as well and slowly climbed to his feet. He held out a hand. "Sorry. I'm Martin Stewart, the baby's father. And you are?"

"Dean Edwards. Your baby's doctor. And Jess's significant other."

What? *What?*

Her entire body suddenly went numb. Dean had just upped the ante from a few casual dates to being involved in a more intimate relationship. Without her permission.

Oh, Lord, she did not want to do this. What if Martin jumped to the conclusion that they were living together?

Except her parents were staying at her house.

Significant other could mean any number of things, though...right?

Her ex was slow to respond, but he finally brought his eyes back to her. "This is a surprise, Jess. Do your folks know?"

Oh, no. Martin had never been great at keeping secrets. And if the way she'd found out about his preference for her sister was anything to go by, her parents were about to get the shock of their lives.

"Please don't say anything. We've been keeping everything kind of hush-hush. I didn't want to take away from Mum and Daddy's anniversary celebration."

"Of course." He glanced down at the baby again. "Can I hold her?"

Well, at least one of the baby's parents wanted to.

Just then the newborn shifted in her arms and stretched, giving a chirping cry. All of her misgivings left in a rush. "She's waking up."

Tiny blue eyes squinted up at them, as if not quite sure what to make of this big new world. Jess leaned over and kissed her little forehead and then carefully stood, minding the tubes and glancing at Dean. "Is it okay?"

"Yes. Just for a moment."

Martin slid into the chair, and Jess carefully placed his baby into his arms. Like the expert he was by now, he rocked her and murmured little endearments, already forgetting anyone else was in the room.

Jess took the opportunity to grab Dean's arm and pull him out of earshot. "What were you thinking?" she whispered.

"Just wanted to reinforce our story. To make sure Abbie bought it."

"Bought it? It's a little over the top, don't you think? What if my parents find out?"

One side of his mouth kicked up. "It wasn't just for Abbie's sake. I wanted to make sure your brother-in-law knew he couldn't go back in time."

"Go back in…" She glanced at Martin and then rolled her eyes. "What is wrong with you people? He's married to my sister. They're happy together."

"Which is why your sister is so worried about what's going on behind her back."

"Nothing. Is. Going. On."

He tugged a stray curl that had gotten loose from her ponytail. "Your sister might just think otherwise. Only now, she and everyone will assume it's going on between you and me."

The man had a point, and she hated him for it. And as soon as the baby was well and on her way home, she and Dean were going to abruptly end their so-called relationship, making sure everyone in her family knew that it was she who'd done the dumping this time.

And as soon as that happened, things could go back to the way they were before. When life was sane…and maybe just the tiniest bit dull.

CHAPTER FIVE

"So WHERE IS HE, and why have we never met him? Or even heard about him?"

The impatience in her mum's voice came through loud and clear. Far from solving all her problems, it seemed she and Dean had stirred up a firestorm. "We've been waiting for years for you to finally decide to invest in something besides your career."

Her jaw tightened. This was the same argument they'd had on many other occasions. They thought she didn't want to get married because she was too busy with her job. Her mum was wrong. Jess did want a family. She wanted to feel as if she belonged to someone as more than a mere shadow of her sister. But she'd never met the right man, and, after Martin, she'd found it much harder to trust than she used to.

It was easier not to argue the point, though. She'd been there and done that, and it had solved nothing.

"I didn't want to ruin your party, Mum."

"Ruin it?" She glanced over at her husband. "We would have had something else to celebrate, right, Norman? Instead, I had to hear about it the day before we return to London. From Martin, no less."

So much for her ex keeping things quiet.

Right now, though, the look in her dad's eyes made her

heart ache. Unlike her mum, her dad had always been the master of giving unconditional love—the type that forgave any transgression. He didn't fuss or join in to castigate her with how she needed to "find a nice boy and settle down". He simply came over and dropped a kiss on her head. "I'm happy for you, love. We both are."

"Oh, Daddy." Unable to stop herself, she threw her arms around his neck and hugged him tight. She couldn't undo what had already been done. Not yet, anyway. Once things died down a bit, she would quietly click that chapter shut and tell her parents it was over between her and Dean.

Somehow.

"So why didn't you say something?" Her mother's crisp voice pulled her back from her father's arms.

She wasn't sure what her mum wanted to hear and was loath to say more than she absolutely had to.

"With the party and Abbie's pregnancy and then…" She shook her head, unable to bring up the painful subject of what had happened at the party. "Well, things have just been hectic."

"We'll want to meet him, of course. It seems your sister and Martin already have." She sat in one of the two slipper chairs in Jess's cottage, her face softening. "Finally. Both of my girls are going to get their happy-ever-afters."

Oh, Mum. Not yet. Not yet.

But she hoped someday she would be as happy as her parents seemed to have been these past thirty years. A lot of that had to do with how easygoing her dad was.

"Tonight." Her mum said the word with a finality that made her blink.

"I'm sorry?"

"I'm going to fix my special shepherd's pie and you'll invite him to dinner. I intend to meet my future son-in-law."

"We're not engaged. We're just..." She took two steps back, horror welling up her throat. This was getting too far out of hand.

"No matter, I want to meet him. What better way than to chat over a meal? Besides, I'm sure he'll eventually propose. Why wouldn't he?"

Um...maybe because he didn't love her. Heavens, how was she going to get out of this?

Her parents had been staying at her little cottage, and her mum had done most of the cooking for the last week and a half. But this? No. She couldn't bring Dean into what could become a powder keg. Even if he had been the one to start it. "Dean probably has to work."

Her mum frowned. "You don't know his rotation schedule?"

Caught in her first lie, she tried to recover. "It's not that I don't know it, it's just that I..."

Don't know.

She did the only thing she could. "I'll ring him and see if he can come." Misery pulled at every word. She was hoping, at the very worst, she could get by with a quick introduction at the hospital along with a smile and a peck on the cheek that was halfway believable. Not a full-blown meal. Where people might actually have to talk. In depth. For hours.

She blamed Dean. And he was going to get an earful the first chance she got.

"Perfect," her mum said, the fingers that had been drumming on the arm of the chair finally going still.

"Why exactly did Martin mention it?"

Her mum smiled. "I heard him and Abbie talking about you, and... Martin let it slip while visiting her room. You know how he is at keeping secrets."

Yes. Unfortunately she did know. All too well. He had barely been able to contain himself when he and Abbie had shown up on her doorstep as a united front. He'd apologized, multiple times, but said he'd fallen in love.

Which was quite funny, considering he'd professed his love to Jess a week before that.

"Ring him now, won't you? Now that we know Marissa Fay is out of the woods, it gives us even more of a reason to get to know your young man."

"He's not my young man, and she's not exactly out of the woods."

Alarm clouded her mother's face. "Did something change?"

"No, Mum, she's doing fine." She couldn't bring herself to put a negative spin on the baby's prognosis just to worm her way out of an uncomfortable situation.

"Well, then?"

Her dad seemed to sense something was afoot, because he laid a hand on his wife's arm. "Gloria, maybe this isn't the time."

Her mum looked closer at her. "You two aren't fighting already, are you?"

No. Because they didn't know each other well enough to argue. Although they'd had a bit of a row at the pub the other evening. "Of course not."

Left with no choice, she pulled her mobile phone out of the pocket of her scrubs, just in time to realize she didn't even know Dean's mobile number… She'd rung his home phone the other times. So she couldn't very well ring him directly.

Damn. Now what did she do? Claim she had no coverage?

No, because one of them could simply check their phone and offer to let her use it. So she did the next best thing.

She pressed the button that would connect her with the hospital's main number. She recognized the woman who answered. Gulping back a bubble of dismay at involving anyone else in this charade, she simply said, "Madeline, this is Jess Black. Would you mind terribly paging Dr. Edwards and asking him to give me a ring?"

"Sure. What's the number?"

Her face heated as she was forced to reel off her mobile number, knowing her mum was going to wonder why Dean wouldn't already have it programmed into his phone. She rang off and swallowed again before turning back to her parents. "He might be with a patient, and I didn't want to disturb him."

Except her mobile buzzed almost immediately. Assuming it was him, she took a deep breath and pressed the button. "Hi, honey."

"Well, hello, there…honey." The low mellow voice on the other end of the line was rife with amusement.

Her teeth clinked together a couple of times before she got up the nerve to continue. "It seems the cat is out of the bag, thanks to you and Martin. He told my parents. About us."

"Ah. I have to admit, I'm a bit disappointed. I thought that 'honey' meant you were actually growing fond of me."

"I am. I mean…well…" She couldn't believe this was happening. Any of it. "Mum and Daddy are leaving *tomorrow*—" she put a subtle emphasis on that word before continuing "—and are anxious to meet you. She thought you might like to have dinner at my place tonight. I told her I wasn't sure of your schedule and that you're extremely busy, so you probably have to work—"

"I would love to come. Tonight, was it?"

"What?" The word came out as a high-pitched squeal, her heart galloping out of control. She'd given him the perfect out, and he'd completely ignored it. Was he that dense? Or was he simply laughing at her discomfiture?

"I said I would love to come to dinner."

Yep. That smug amusement was still there, coloring every word he spoke.

He was getting his jollies at her predicament, was he? A predicament he'd helped create.

"You're sure you don't *have to work*?" She was a little less subtle this time.

"Positive. I'm off duty. Free as a bird."

Damn him.

"I guess that works perfectly, then. Six-ish?" She glanced toward her mother, who nodded before reaching for her father's hand and gripping it tight, her own triumph evident.

Time to make Dean pay a little bit for not bowing out. "I'll save the story of how we met, then, for tonight. I know how much you adore telling that funny bit about the lake. About how you fell in, and I had to rescue you."

"Brat."

"No more than you…honey."

"I'll see you tonight. I take it I have carte blanche on that story, then?"

She had a feeling that not only had the cat been let out of the bag, but the genie had just been released from the bottle. "I trust you to stick to the pertinent points."

"Always. I need to go—I still have a few patients to see." There was a pause, then he came back. "I guess I'll see you tonight, sweetheart."

Ack! Even though she knew he was just trying to make her fidget—and he was doing a good job of that—the words still made a funny little pinging happen in the center of her chest. She decided to ignore it. Especially since she was the one who'd started the whole endearment thing.

"See you tonight." As she hurried to mash the button to cut off the call, she could have sworn it ended with Dean's laughter.

Despite the way he'd teased her on the phone, Dean wasn't all that sure about doing this dinner thing tonight. But he'd given his word. He pulled into the driveway of a small cottage, then checked the address again. This was the place.

The beige paint with its crisp white gingerbread trim reminded him so much of Jess that it made him smile. He couldn't see the sister living in a minuscule place like this, but Jess? Absolutely. This fit her to a tee. And the image of coming home to something like this...of that sturdy wooden door opening and a couple of happy kids rushing down the walkway to greet him, made a pang go through his gut. It would be so very different from the loneliness and never-ending fear he'd experienced as a child.

As if by magic, the door did open. But it wasn't children who stood there, but the woman he'd just been sitting here thinking about.

Jess. Dressed in jeans that were tucked into brown boots and a long beige sweater that hugged her curves, she looked homey and, oh, so different from the way she dressed for work. She was as quaint and welcoming as the cottage. Except for that nervous frown.

Over their little deception? *His* little deception. He was to blame for this entire thing, and he could see it wasn't going to be without consequences.

He'd put Jess into an untenable position. No one wanted to lie to their parents. But her sister had pushed just the right buttons, and he'd instinctively stepped in between her and Jess in a figurative sense. If he'd had more time, he might have come up with something a little less drastic though.

Which brought up another point. Were Jess's parents so unused to seeing her with a man that they assumed this was something special? From the way she'd acted about their bet a few days ago, maybe that was indeed the case.

Staring. He was staring.

Clicking open the door to his car, he exited, giving her a little salute as he retrieved something from the passenger seat. Two sets of flowers. One for Jess and one for her mum. No need to make anyone suspect things weren't what they seemed in paradise.

He'd never bought a woman flowers in his life, not wanting anyone to think he planned on sticking around after a night or two.

But this was safe, right? Jess knew it was all a charade. Easily ended. Once her parents and her sister left, that would be that.

He made it up to the front door, making sure his eyes stayed glued to her face, no matter how much they might want to roam over that delectable figure. Once he arrived, though, and handed her one set of flowers, he glanced behind her and noted her mum was watching from a few yards behind Jess.

What better excuse to...?

He placed one hand on her shoulders and squeezed slightly, watching her eyes widen and her nostrils flare as he drew close and pressed his lips to hers, allowing his mouth to graze across them and then continue along her cheek.

She shivered as he reached her ear, and he couldn't hold back a smile. "Relax," he whispered. "Mum is watching."

With that, he released her, waiting for her to step back. Which she did, but it was in a stumbling rush that had him reaching out to grip her wrist to steady her. He threaded his fingers through hers to keep her next to him. He had a feeling all she wanted to do was disappear into the inner depths of the house. Not something a woman in a serious relationship would do.

He tugged her closer as he turned his smile onto the woman who looked so much like her. "Mrs. Black. Thank you again for inviting me." He held out the second bouquet, watching her smile as she accepted it with a look that might have been relief.

"Please call me Gloria. I can't tell you how glad I am to hear that you and Jess are together." Her smile reached her eyes this time. "I'll just go put these in water. Would you like something to drink?"

"Just a glass of wine, please. Red, if you have it."

Gloria looked confused for a second, then Jess cleared her throat. "I don't keep alcohol in the house, Dean, remember?"

Bloody hell. That was something he should know. "Of course. I should have brought a bottle with me. How thoughtless."

"It's fine." If anything, Jess's voice was even tighter. "It's better for Daddy not to have it sitting at the table, anyway."

A chill went through him. Jess's dad was an alcoholic?

Memories of his own father's battle went through his head. Only his fight hadn't just been against the bottle. It had been against his wife and son once he'd slugged down his nightly quota and lost sight of his soul, or whatever it was that had kept the hounds of hell at bay.

Once released, they'd slashed and torn at everything within reach.

Had Jess experienced any of that horror?

From the look on her face, that would be a no. So her dad wasn't a mean drunk.

"My grandfather," she said in a low voice as her mum turned to go back into the kitchen. "He abused my dad and his other kids until he died of cirrhosis. Daddy doesn't want anything to do with alcohol, so none of us drink in front of him."

That was funny because Dean allowed himself the occasional drink for the exact opposite reason: to prove he could control his usage when his father hadn't been able to.

Speaking of control…

"Your grandfather never hurt *you*, did he?" There was a tension in Dean's jaw that he didn't like. Images running through his head that he liked even less.

"He died before I was born." She touched his arm. "Daddy's nothing like him. Please don't mention any of this."

Not a chance. He never talked about his own parents. To anyone. He'd buried that part of him so deep it rarely ever came to the surface anymore. Except at times like this. Unlike Jess's grandfather, his dad was still very much alive. At least he thought he was. He hadn't spoken to the man since the day he went to prison. In fact, he hadn't heard from his mum in a long time either. This was the first time he'd thought of either of them in years.

Damn.

A mixture of churning emotions boiled up from somewhere inside, threatening to reach the surface.

The sooner he got out of there, the better. He didn't want to accidentally say something at the table that might bring back painful memories. For Jess's dad. For himself.

Her dad came out of the kitchen wearing a ruffled apron that could only belong to his daughter. The queasy sensation stalled, and then subsided.

"Sorry for the frilly gear," the other man said. "I've been telling Jess she needs to buy some gender-neutral things if I'm to do much cooking."

Dean brushed the words aside with a smile, reaching out to shake her father's hand. His grip was solid, putting Dean at ease almost immediately. He wasn't the alcoholic. But he had experienced what it was like to be at one's mercy.

They had something in common. And he got the feeling that Jess's father would have kept his family safe from anyone or anything that threatened it.

"Norman Black. Nice to meet you."

"You as well. I'm Dean Edwards."

Jess made a little sound in her throat, hands gripped tightly together. "So what are we having?"

"Shepherd's pie, remember? Your mum did the majority of the work tonight. I simply made the salad."

Shrugging out of his coat when Jess reached toward it, Dean let her hang it up by the front door, where several others were—one he recognized as the coat she'd worn to the Indian restaurant and to the pub. With a quick flick she draped his over the top of that very one.

A peculiar flash of awareness crept up his spine. He shot her a glance to see if she'd done that on purpose, but she was already moving farther into the room, laughing at something her dad had said. He threw another look at the winter gear and then shrugged. They were just coats. Not a metaphor for anything else.

"I think Mum is ready." She was back at his side. "I hope you like shepherd's pie." There was an uncertainty to her voice that made him take a closer look.

"Adore it. My mum didn't seem to…"

He'd almost said that his mother didn't like to cook, unless she knew her husband was on his way home. And that was only because she knew what would happen if dinner wasn't on the table when he arrived.

"She didn't seem to…?"

"Nothing. She was just never keen on fixing things that didn't come from a tin."

"Did she work?"

He shook his head, blasting himself for even going there. And he wasn't sure why he had. There was just something about Jess that invited confidences, shared secrets…and aroused his protective instincts, evidently.

Besides, hadn't she just finished sharing a pretty big secret of her own—about her grandfather's drinking? It was human nature to want to mirror what someone else did.

He wasn't quite satisfied with that explanation, but, since they were now in Jess's minuscule dining room, he didn't have time to formulate any other theories.

And his growling stomach reminded him that he'd skipped lunch. Something smelled delicious.

Right on cue, Gloria hurried out of the kitchen. "Jess, would you put some ice in the glasses and get the drinks ready please?"

"Is there anything I can help with?" he asked.

She waved him away. "No, just have a seat. I've put you to the left of where Jess normally sits."

Another thing he didn't know about her. Before he had to guess, Jess went around the table and picked up a glass. "What would you like to drink? Something fizzy?"

Okay, so that was where he was to sit. *Thank you, Jess.*

"Just give me whatever you're having."

Soon they were all situated around the table. Needing a drink of something stronger than the water he'd been served, he sucked down a mouthful, only to have bubbles assault his throat. He swallowed in a hurry, fighting the need to cough. Losing.

Jess laughed. "I wondered why you wanted tonic water. You normally hate it."

He jerked around to stare at her before realizing she'd simply hazarded a guess. She didn't know he hated it. Or why. There was no way she could know that when his father had sat at the dinner table guzzling whatever his liquor du jour had been, a too young Dean—wanting to be like his dad—had begged his mum for whatever his father was drinking. She'd served him tonic water, instead, and pretended it was the real thing. By the time he'd been old enough to know what was going on and to equate the drinking with the abuse, he'd hated his "grown up" drink.

He was not about to admit that now, though. So he took another sip, albeit a more cautious one this time, forcing the cold fizzy liquid to sit in his mouth for a second before swallowing it down in a rush. "Just trying to develop a taste for it, that's all."

Something that was never going to happen.

Gloria reached for his plate and placed a generous portion of the meat pie on it. "Well, isn't that sweet? That's true love for you. I can't tell you the number of things that Norm has learned to like for me."

Another pang went through Dean's chest. This was what love was supposed to be like. Unfortunately, it didn't usually work out that way. Look at his folks. Or even Jess's sister and her husband, for that matter. Fighting and bickering seemed to come with the territory. As did problems like drinking and abuse and jealousy.

No, thanks. He was glad he'd steered clear of all that. His life was fine just the way it was.

Jess took his plate from her mum and put it in front of him. Then she covered his hand with hers. "Dean does all kinds of nice things for me. Don't you, honey?"

He almost choked again, but not because he had anything in his mouth. It was because of the image that suddenly went through his head. He *could* do all kinds of nice things for her, if she let him.

Not going to happen.

Not in this lifetime. And not in the next. Besides, he'd tried to take her home for a fun-filled night of sex, only to have her turn him down flat. Something Dean wasn't used to. It still stung to remember the way her eyes had sparkled with anger as she'd turned and walked away from him.

Although as she started to withdraw her hand her fingers slid along his in a way that made his skin heat and caused certain muscles to tighten in warning. Had she done that on purpose?

Before he could think it through, he turned his hand over and stopped her fingers from leaving his, smiling when he heard her soft intake of breath.

She wanted to play games, did she? She had no idea who she was dealing with. He was a tactical expert when it came to this kind of war. "I love doing things for you." He put a wealth of meaning into those words, smiling when sudden color flared along her cheekbones and slid into her hairline.

Her mum's brows went up. She'd certainly gotten it.

"I have to admit, Jess, I'd almost given up hope. I'm so glad you've decided that work isn't all there is to life." She handed a plate to Norman. "They're almost as cheeky as we were at their age."

Cheeky wasn't exactly the word he would use. Lustful. Needy. Wanting. Those were all terms that described him right now.

He wanted her. In spite of the fact that she didn't seem to want him in return.

They were simply playing a part. A part that would end the second her family went home to London.

But that didn't stop him from wishing he could take her back to his place and see just how far they could take this little charade.

"We were, weren't we?" her dad said.

Jess tugged at her hand, and this time he let her go. Besides her mum was now dishing out the rest of their food and making sure everyone had what they needed.

Not by a long shot. But this was the hand he'd been dealt. And from where he was standing, it looked as if two things needed to happen. One, he needed to get laid. Two, Jess needed a whopping dose of self-confidence. Maybe they should both head back to the pub and grab the first available partner to satisfy those needs. Except they'd already tried that and it hadn't worked. He was actually lucky she'd turned him down, because Dean didn't date people from work. Ever. Too messy. Too complicated. He preferred things simple and to the point.

Jess was neither.

So yeah, his moment of weakness that night at the pub could have turned into a major disaster.

Digging into his food to take his mind off Jess, he wasn't surprised at how good it tasted. What did surprise him, though, was how comfortable her father seemed to be in the kitchen. None of this expecting one person to get everything to the table while the other slouched on the sofa doing nothing.

"Delicious. Thank you so much for inviting me."

"I just wish Jess would have told us about you sooner." Gloria sent her daughter a look of reproof.

"Nothing to tell." Jess half muttered the words.

Her mother either didn't hear her or was ignoring her. "So tell us a little about yourself, Dean."

This time it was Dean who stiffened. He'd expected to be asked about the "falling into the lake" story Jess had threatened him with over the phone. Not something about himself personally. "What would you like to know?"

"Are you as fixated on your job as Jess is?"

"Mum, please." Jess sounded miserable.

Hoping to defuse the situation, he said, "I think most medical professionals are pretty dedicated."

Norman covered his wife's hand with his own. "Of course they are. When did you realize you wanted to be a doctor?"

When? The day he decided he wanted to help *fix* people instead of breaking them. But he wasn't about to say that. "I think it's every child's dream at some point. With me, it just seemed to stick."

"And you and Jess met at the hospital?"

This time it was his daughter who answered. "Yes. We work in different wards, but see each other from time to time."

Yes, they did. Except that Jess hadn't expected Dean to even know who she was. There was something about that that bothered him. Really bothered him.

He'd joked about her invisibility cloak, but now he wondered. Did she really think she was that invisible? He'd noticed her from the time she'd started working at Cambridge Royal four years ago. The way her blonde ponytail swished from side to side as she walked. The way she had of lifting a hand to wave at colleagues instead of simply nodding to them.

The way she smiled as she looked down at her patients.

He'd noticed all of that? When?

He realized everyone was staring at him. "Sorry?"

"My dad asked what our most romantic date was."

The sardonic tilt of her brow told him he really should have thought this through a little better, or at least planned for the obvious questions. Hmm…well, they wanted romantic? He would give them romantic.

"Well, after the 'falling in the lake' bit that Jess mentioned, we seemed to hit it off. I think our most memorable afternoon was when I took her for a nice little hack in the countryside. Just the two of us on horseback. We took a hamper of food. And—"

"You took her out for a hack?" Her dad interrupted him, and he could have sworn the steady gaze now held a hint of suspicion.

And Jess. Well, she looked just plain horrified. He had a feeling he was about to find out why.

Gloria took up where Norm left off. "Jess is afraid of horses. Has been ever since she was thrown from a pony when she was young."

"I—I got over it. Dean helped me see there's really nothing to be afraid of." Except she looked pretty afraid right now.

Perfect. He had to choose the one thing Jess was terrified of, and her dad had called him on it.

"Well I, for one, would love to see some pictures of that. Wouldn't you?" Norm's question was aimed at Jess's mum.

"Definitely."

He and Jess had two choices. They could either come clean and tell the truth—which meant her sister might start back up with the accusations—or he could continue to do his best to make this look real.

"I don't have any of those shots with me at the moment." His mind scrambled to find a solution. "I know you're leaving tomorrow—perhaps I could email them to you?"

"Perfect. We'll be expecting them." There was definitely an edge to the words this time.

Jess glanced at him, a frown on her face, but she didn't contradict him. Instead, she said, "I'll have Dean send them to me, and then I'll forward them to you. How does that sound?" She dropped her fork onto her almost empty plate. "Well, I need to save room for some of that delicious custard tart you made, Mum."

The rest of the evening revolved around small talk and chatter about some of the cases they'd worked on. Somehow, though, he didn't think her dad was going to forget about those pictures. Which meant he and Jess were going to have to do some creative maneuvering. Like editing a photo to show her on a horse?

No. That wouldn't work.

He was going to have to actually get her on one and snap a few pictures.

And if he couldn't talk her into it?

Well, he was going to have to, because if they didn't do something and fast his impulsive decision was going to wind up coming back and biting him right on the ass. Which would be fine, if it were only him. But he didn't want Jess to pay the price for his mistakes.

No, he was going to have to sweet talk her into agreeing. And unlike at the pub a few nights ago, he was going to have to make sure she said yes.

CHAPTER SIX

"You want me to do what?"

Surely Jess hadn't heard him correctly. Dean wanted her to get on a horse? Her dad was right. She was afraid of horses. Terrified of them. They were huge and all kinds of scary.

"Just for a couple of pictures."

"I think I'd rather just tell my parents we've decided not to see each other anymore."

Dean leaned against the door of his car as they stood in front of Jess's house. Dinner had actually gone quite well, except for that one hiccup. "Your sister will still be in town after they leave, I assume. Are you going to tell her we broke up as well?"

She closed her eyes. If she did that, she could almost guarantee the arguments would start right back up. And Abbie would probably claim that she'd broken things off with Dean because she was still secretly in love with Martin. They would be back to square one. Unless she and Dean could keep up the pretense until her sister left.

When would that be?

"I really am afraid of them."

"I know this bloke—"

"This *bloke*? Well, that certainly puts my mind at ease."

Dean grinned and reached for one of her hands, threading his fingers through hers. "How about if I promise to ask him for a very nice horse?"

"Is there such a thing?" She rolled her eyes. "Why didn't you just tell my dad you'd taken me to the Bull Run in Spain? Or that we'd done the polar plunge while visiting Russia? Those would be more believable than the idea of me on a horse."

"It would be a little harder to get photographs of one of those events, don't you think?" He carried her hand to his mouth, placing a kiss on her knuckles that made her stiffen. "For your dad's benefit. I don't think he's fully bought into our little love story."

"This was such a huge mistake." She glanced toward the front window of the cottage, just the same. Were her parents really watching them to see if they were truly dating each other? She'd sensed some definite tension from her dad, but assumed it was the normal protective instincts that most fathers had for their daughters. He'd certainly been angry enough at Martin when he'd switched his attentions to Abbie.

"You've already gotten through the hardest part," Dean continued. "Having dinner with them."

"Really? You're not the one who has to get on the back of a crazed animal and hope it decides to let you live."

If anything, his smile grew. "You're being a bit melodramatic, don't you think? We'll climb on a couple of docile horses and take a few snapshots. It'll be over before you know it."

"Is that what you tell your patients?"

He tugged her closer, until she found herself up against him, his hands at her hips. "My patients are too little to understand anything except a cuddle and a full tummy."

The image of Dean cradling one of those tiny preemies made her heart squeeze. He would make a fantastic dad, if he could ever get past the need to jump from one woman to another.

She just had to make sure he remembered this was strictly make-believe.

Before she could say anything, though, his nose nuzzled the skin just below her ear. Electricity shimmered along her nerve endings. "Dean, what are you doing?"

Her voice came out far too shaky for her liking.

"Your dad is standing at the window watching us," he whispered.

"He is?" Her instinct was to crank her head around again and look at the house. Instead, she found a palm cupping her chin and holding her in place.

"Trust me. He's there." His lips touched her cheek, and this time instead of the hum of electricity, her muscles reacted with a violent shudder that swept from her toes to the top of her head. "It's just a pretend hack. We'll stay close to the barn. I promise."

"I...I..." Her thoughts were careening around in her head—a terrifying mixture of fear and need, each vying for supremacy. "I guess I can try."

"That's my girl." He brushed his nose against hers. "In the meantime, let's give your father something to ponder while he waits for those pictures."

With that, his lips slid against hers. Once. Twice.

It's just pretend.

And then, proving she didn't really believe that at all, she reached up on tiptoes and pressed her mouth hard against his.

Dean went totally still for all of five seconds, then his arms wrapped around her waist and he hauled her tight against him, head tilting. Suddenly the pretend kiss became something that was very, very real. And she had no idea how to stop it. Or if she even wanted to.

* * *

This situation had turned on its head so completely it wasn't funny. The last thing Dean would have ordinarily wanted was for the father of one of his dates to catch him necking with his daughter. But this was no ordinary situation.

And neither was this kiss.

Dean didn't care who was watching him, because with Jess's arms wound around his neck and her lips open beneath his there was a raw primitive feel he never would have associated with this particular woman.

Her ex had given this up? For someone Dean had come to view as a shrew?

His hand cupped the base of her skull and turned her head just slightly. Just enough for him to really settle his mouth against hers.

Well, Daddy dearest would probably not need those pictures after seeing this.

Except he *wanted* to take Jess to his friend's stable. Wanted her to be willing to try something different, to do something wild and crazy and maybe even a little terrifying.

Like this kiss?

Definitely. His tongue surged forward, finding no resistance at all, just a warm moist place he never wanted to leave.

And damn if she didn't make this sexy little sound in the back of her throat. The one that whispered for him to keep going, to press her hard against the side of the car and take it all the way to the finish line.

Somehow he didn't think her dad would be as kosher with him doing his daughter right here in the garden, no matter how much Dean might want to.

So he eased her back, a curse running through his mind. Rippling through his body.

Her lips remained slightly parted, her breath coming in and out in cute little gusts that made him want to drag her into the bushes and finish what he'd started.

He leaned his weight against the car door, pressing his forehead against hers. "You okay?"

"Huh?" Slowly her arm unwound from his neck. "Oh. Um…yes. Fine."

She didn't sound fine. Her voice trembled and there was a quality to it that made him wonder exactly how often she'd been caught necking in front of her dad.

Probably never, from the sound of it. Her mum's comment about Jess being all work and no play…was that based on reality?

Hell, he wasn't thinking straight right now.

Blowing out a breath, he stroked the back of his fingers along her cheek. "As good as that was, I'd rather leave with all of my teeth intact."

Jess tilted her head for a second, and then, as if realizing what he was talking about, gave a nervous chuckle. "I don't think he would knock them *all* out."

The woman was a complete enigma. The unexpected heat of that kiss had hit him right between the eyes. And then her shy teasing afterward brought out every protective instinct he possessed. If he'd been her dad, he'd have come down that pavement like a raging bull, pulling Dean off her and sending him on his way.

Releasing her, he leaned forward and gave her cheek a quick kiss, finding it warm from her blush.

Or maybe from her reaction to finding herself in his arms.

Back away, Dean.

Maybe it would have been better to have saved this part of the act for her sister and brother-in-law.

He could always do it again.

That thought made something curl low in his gut. Some warm anticipation that made him plan crazy, impulsive things.

Impulsive…like his father?

That kiss had certainly blown out of control far too quickly.

But he hadn't hurt her. Or anyone else.

He forced himself to say it again. "Are you okay?"

"Yes." She nodded and took a step back, pushing her hair back from her face. "Yes, I think I am."

It sounded as if she'd just been handed a revelation. But what kind of revelation? Of how good it felt to be thoroughly kissed in front of your house? Or that she never wanted to repeat it?

He already knew which side he was camped on. The do-it-again-soon camp.

"So you'll let me know if we need to nudge your dad in the right direction again."

"And what direction would that be?"

"Toward believing this—" he motioned between the two of them "—is real."

It had felt real to him. A little too real.

She shook her head. "If he doesn't believe it by now, I don't know what more we can do to convince him."

There was no way he was going to touch that. Because if he did, he'd tell her to slide into his car and he'd take her somewhere and show her.

"Pictures. We still need pictures."

Yes. That was the answer he was looking for.

"I don't know…"

He reached out to slide his thumb along her cheekbone. "No getting out of it now."

"Okay."

Her capitulation had happened far too easily. Or maybe she was still as stunned as he was by what had happened between them.

Whatever it was, she was keeping it to herself, because she took two more steps back, and then, with a murmured goodbye, turned and headed up the walk. Sure enough, he was positive the edge of one of her lacy curtains had just dropped back into place as her dad…or maybe her mum… decided the show was over.

And yet, the energy in his body was still humming with possibility.

Even though that possibility was now opening the door and going inside her house.

A day later, and despite her best efforts, Martin finally cornered her in the hospital corridor. She'd just finished a difficult delivery and was hoping to call her friend Amy and remind her that she was due for a checkup, since she'd missed her last appointment.

He stood in front of her, not exactly blocking her path, but almost. "I know all of this has been tough on you— not to mention Gloria and Norm—and I wanted to say I'm sorry for how Abs is acting. She's not herself at the moment."

Hmm…her sister hadn't "been herself" since they were teenagers. Surely there were other twins who weren't best friends. "She's in a strange hospital with caregivers who aren't her own. It's natural for her to feel out of sorts."

"She's taking it out on you, though. And for that I'm sorry."

"Don't be. She's worried about the baby." In reality,

that was what Jess hoped it was, although Abbie hadn't shown quite as much interest in this child as she had when her other three had been born. She'd doted over each of those in turn.

But she'd barely visited Marissa while she'd been in hospital, even though her room was just down the hall from the SCBU. Martin, on the other hand, had been a constant figure there, ever since his arrival in Cambridge, even getting to know the nurses and speaking with Dean on several occasions. That made her nervous. One slip and Dean could make the situation between her and her sister that much worse. The last thing she needed was for Abbie to start back in on her about her ex.

Dean's plan had worked. So far.

But it hadn't made Abbie want to spend any more time with the baby.

"She's had a traumatic experience," Jess continued. "Maybe she just needs some time to heal physically and emotionally.

Could her sister be suffering from some form of PTSD? That hardly seemed likely, but maybe her blaming Jess for the premature birth was a way of making herself feel better. In reality, neither of them was to blame. At least Jess kept telling herself that.

And so did Dean. On a regular basis.

He'd stuck by her side with a glue-like tenacity that made her edgy. In fact, she was surprised he hadn't popped out of the woodwork by now with some murmured endearment—although she did notice he was careful around the nurses and staff, for which she was grateful. Because the monikers he chose for her were peculiar. Especially one of them, which made her squirm.

My girl.

She was not "his" and never would be. The first time

he'd said it—in front of her house when she'd agreed to climb on a horse—she'd passed it off as a "good girl" kind of thing. But it seemed the words had stuck. In his defense, she had called him honey. But she'd done that with a sardonic edge.

There was nothing humorous about the term he was using.

And she wished with all her might he would stop. Wasn't there something called a self-fulfilling prophesy? She didn't want to start believing those words could, should, or would become true. Ever.

Martin's voice reminded her of his presence. "Where's Dean? Maybe he could talk to Abbie. Or maybe even prescribe her something."

The thought of Dean going and talking to Abbie alone made something in her cringe, even though it was ridiculous. Old fears, however, were hard to banish.

But if she was worried that Abbie was going to try to flirt with Dean, she needn't bother. Dean wasn't hers.

That's my girl.

For some reason, she didn't think Dean would have ever done what Martin had done. Why she thought that she had no idea. Martin had been the last boyfriend she'd lost to Abbie, but he hadn't been the only one.

Dean's not your boyfriend, fiancé, significant other or anything else. Not really.

Abbie couldn't steal something Jess had never had.

"I think that's something you should discuss with Dean and Abbie, not me."

A voice came from behind her. "What should I discuss?"

Jess whirled around to find the man in question standing just behind her, his brown hair rumpled as if he'd run his fingers through it many times. His eyes looked tired. In fact, he looked flat-out exhausted.

"Hard day?" The words had come out before she'd had a chance to think things through.

"Pretty bad." He reached down to link one of his fingers with her, making her tense up. "I just want to settle down on the couch with a cuppa and you."

Ugh. He was laying it on pretty thick. She'd almost gotten used to his teasing over the last day or two, maybe because he restricted it to when they were around her family. But maybe she should talk to him about easing up. "I think Martin wanted to talk to you about Abbie."

Martin's face had slowly infused with red as they'd stood there. "It's not important. It can wait for another time."

"But Abbie—"

"Just needs some time to recover. Rest. You said it yourself."

Dean tilted his head. "Is something worrying you? I can take a quick look before I head out."

"It can wait until tomorrow." He looked as if he was going to turn around and leave, but then he took a deep breath. "I held the baby for a while today. She seemed more alert."

"She's getting stronger."

Martin's eyes closed for a second. "Thank God. I'll be sure to tell Abbie."

"Has she been down there yet today?" Dean voiced what Jess had been thinking.

"No. Not today. Maybe tomorrow." Martin's voice didn't sound any more sure than Jess's had been when she'd gone to visit her sister today.

Not that she'd said much. To her, anyway.

Unwilling to let Martin walk away without her saying something, she pulled her hand from Dean's grip and touched her ex's sleeve. "You've got my mobile number if you need me, right?"

He nodded. "Yes. And, Jess…" There was a short pause. "Thank you for everything."

"You're welcome."

With that he started back down the hall toward her sister's room.

When she turned to face Dean again, he looked even less happy than he had a few minutes ago.

"What?"

"Should you be doing that?"

Confusion made her blink. "Doing what?"

"Encouraging him to ring you."

"Is there a reason why I shouldn't?"

He took a step closer. "I would think that would be obvious. Your sister is already suspicious. Asking him to ring your mobile…"

He thought she was encouraging him in a romantic way?

Confusion turned to anger. Why did everyone assume she was up to no good? Her sister. Her mum, during the party. And now Dean. "I only asked him to ring if he needed something." She swallowed when that didn't come out quite right and tried again. "If he or *Abbie* needed something, or if he was concerned about the baby. Besides, my whole family now believes we're a couple. Thanks to you."

"You seemed happy enough to go along with it at the time."

She had been. But she was thinking more and more that this had been a mistake. It would be in everyone's best interest to get those pictures, show them off to her family, and then go back to seeing Dean as little as possible. Which made her wonder why he'd wandered down to her part of the hospital in the first place. "Was there something you wanted?"

"As a matter of fact, yes. I spoke with my friend. The one with the horses. And he said we can come over anytime. We just need to let him know so that he can have our horses tacked up and ready to go."

Ready to go. She doubted she would ever be ready. But she could do this. If she could survive her sister's betrayal and now her accusations, she could surely survive sitting on a horse for a few seconds. It would be over before she knew it.

Ugh. Weren't those the same words that Dean had used? Right before he'd called her "his girl".

"I have the next couple of days off, so maybe the sooner we do this, the better." She glanced at his face, again wondering at the tired lines beside his mouth. "Did something happen with a patient?"

"No. Just had some personal issues come up."

Personal. As in another woman?

Oh, great. She hadn't thought of that. That she might be cramping his style as far as his love life was concerned. "If you want to go out with someone, I don't want to stand—"

One side of his mouth went up. "It's not a woman. Although it might be a hell of a lot easier if it were."

She flinched. As hard as she'd tried to remain stock-still, those words had hit her hard.

"Hey." He wrapped warm fingers around her upper arm and edged her down the hallway until he came to an unoccupied room. He ducked inside, still towing her behind him.

"I don't understand."

"I don't suppose you do." He looked torn, as if part of

him wanted to explain what was going on and the other part didn't.

"It's my father," he finally said. "It appears he's just been released from prison. They've lost track of him and are afraid he might show up here at the hospital."

CHAPTER SEVEN

HE WASN'T SURE why he'd told Jess about his father. Maybe because he wanted her to be prepared if the man suddenly burst into the hospital looking for him.

Damn. The last thing he wanted to see was that part of his past. It was also the last thing he wanted Jess to see. In spite of the tension between her and her twin, Jess's home life was so…normal. Her mum seemed a little prickly at times, but her parents had been married for thirty years, for God's sake. And he'd bet his life that her father had never once lifted a hand to his wife or daughters.

Flipping a pencil into the cup on his desk, he felt as if he was caught in a vat of quicksand. Telling her had probably been a mistake. And yet if he hadn't…

Did he even know what his father looked like after all these years? No. But if he knew the man, one of the first things he'd do was head for the nearest pub. After that…

He stood. It would do no good at all to sit here and brood. He'd arrived early to work this morning so that he would be able to leave early and take Jess to the horse stable, and then they were off to an ice-skating rink that wasn't far from where his friend lived. Maybe between the stable and swirling around on the ice, her family would believe they were indeed a pair.

And he'd bet that Jess could use a break.

Speaking of Jess's sister, he wanted to make a quick stop at the SCBU and see how Marissa was doing this morning. He made it halfway down the hall and caught sight of Abbie at the nurses' desk talking with one of the special-care nurses. Deidre…perfect.

Abbie half turned toward him and her mouth shut in a hurry, the pink hue that was so common to Jess's cheeks seeping into Abbie's. Did she not want him to hear their conversation?

If so, it was none of his business. Except Deidre was also staring at him.

He nodded at her as he arrived, only to have her nod back and then hurry away. Abbie was now fidgeting with her sweater.

That was right. She'd been released from hospital as of this morning. He'd only seen her in a hospital gown until now. She appeared a little softer somehow. More human.

Looks could be deceiving, however.

"How is the baby?"

Abbie glanced at her hands, which were splayed across the nurse's desk. "I was heading there now. Do you want to walk with me?"

Dean immediately went on alert, but covered it with a smile. "I was going there as well. Shall we?"

He dropped into step beside Abbie and waited for whatever she wanted to say. Because it was pretty obvious something was on her mind.

It didn't take long.

"I think I may have let the cat out of the bag."

Every muscle inside of him went taut with tension. Had Jess told Abbie about his father and the worry that he might come to the hospital? He hoped not. It wasn't exactly something he wanted broadcast through the gossip chain. He still wasn't even sure why he'd told Jess about it.

Maybe because his first reaction was to protect those he cared about from whatever his father might do.

Which meant what? That he cared for Jess?

Of course he did. As a friend and as a colleague.

So why hadn't he told Deidre or any of his other work acquaintances?

He ignored the question and focused on Abbie. "And what might you have let out of the bag?"

"I happened to mention you were dating my sister to a couple of the nurses, and they seemed surprised."

Relief washed over him. As bad as that was, it seemed a whole lot better than everyone finding out about his father or his childhood.

His focus narrowed. Actually it wasn't better. And he was pretty sure Jess would agree with him. "We were trying to keep that quiet, actually."

She nodded. "I guess I realize that now, from people's reactions. But I... I was just so surprised that Jess was actually seeing someone that it just came out."

Did she really expect him to believe that? Or was she fishing for information, as Jess's dad had seemed to do. And what could he use for an excuse? It came to him just as they reached the door of the special-care nursery. "We haven't made things official yet, so I didn't want her to be bombarded by a thousand questions."

"I guess I can understand that." Abbie's voice held more than a tinge of curiosity.

They arrived at the SCBU and he held open the door and waited for her to go in. She had the grace to look slightly sheepish. "I won't say anything else, then."

"Thank you." He eyed her. "Let me help you hold your baby."

"Oh, but…" Her voice died away as if she couldn't really think of a good excuse to refuse.

What was wrong with her? His mum had never been very maternal, but he'd always assumed that was because she'd lived in fear for so many years. Had his life really started out like this? Had his mum been at all eager to hold him as a child? She'd never had any other kids.

Well, this baby was going to get at least one good cuddle from her mother before she left the hospital.

"There's a chair right in front of her cot. If you'll slide into one of those gowns hanging on the pegs and then get yourself settled, I'll check her over and then let you hold her."

"Very well. Let's make it quick, shall we?"

Dean frowned. Jess might let her sister run roughshod over her, but Dean was not about to let her do it to him. He took his time checking the baby's color and checking the obs the nurse had posted on the chart. Abbie and Martin's baby was very lucky. She was strong and healthy. Too small to be released, but there was no reason to think she wouldn't go on to have a very normal life.

Glancing to the side, he noted that Abbie had donned the requisite gown and was perched on the very edge of the plastic chair. "Go ahead and scoot back so that you're comfortable before you hold her. It'll be a lot more difficult for you to get settled once she's in your arms."

Abbie pushed herself to the very back of the chair. She didn't look more comfortable, though. That was neither here nor there as far as he was concerned.

Carefully opening the top of the special cot, he checked the wires and tubes to make sure nothing was tangled, then, sliding one gloved hand beneath the baby's neck to support it and the other beneath her nappy, he lifted her up, holding her close to his body and absorbing that quintessential baby smell as he pivoted on his heel. Abbie was still sitting exactly as she had been…hands clasped together in her lap.

"Hold out your arms, and I'll place her in them."

There was a pause of two or three seconds before she actually did as he requested. "Ready?"

She gave a curt nod.

Dean set the baby into the crook of Abbie's left arm and waited to make sure she had her before moving away.

"She doesn't look like him." Her voice was small. Quiet. So quiet he thought he must have misunderstood her.

"I'm sorry?"

"Nothing." She seemed to come to herself. "Babies don't always look like their parents when they're this small, after all."

"Not always. No." A sense of foreboding rose up. Something was wrong with this picture, but he had no idea what it was. When Jess had held the baby, it had seemed so natural. She'd looked down at her niece with such an expression of love that it had taken his breath away. There was none of that emotional vibe with Abbie. In fact, she seemed almost repelled.

Kind of like his mum had been with him?

But Abbie had other children. Children she seemed to love dearly.

It wasn't up to him to understand anything except the physical health of these tiny, helpless beings.

Deidre poked her head into the room. "Dr. Edwards? One of Dr. Granger's patients has eclampsia. She's not due for almost three months. They're asking for you."

"Are they inducing?"

"Her blood pressure is too high. They're going to take the baby now."

The sense of foreboding he'd had a moment ago was

nothing compared to the way his heart jerked and sprinted at a rate that he recognized.

Far too early. If they were going to take the baby it meant the mum's life was in imminent danger. His job was to do what he could for the baby. "Tell them I'm on my way."

Deidre ducked back out of the room.

"You can't leave me here alone with her!" The panicked voice came from the chair.

Abbie. And she sounded more than dismayed. She sounded petrified.

He glanced down and saw he was right. Her eyes were wide with fear, her tense fingers tightening on Marissa's tiny frame.

"I'll send the nurse back in. I'm sorry, but I have to go." Giving her no further chance to object, he turned and headed out of the door. He asked Deidre to check in on Abbie as he went down the hall.

When he arrived at the surgical suite he shoved his arms through a gown and scrubbed in. The interior of the room held the sort of ordered chaos he'd come to expect. As his mind picked apart what was what, he saw that he'd arrived just as obstetrical surgeon Sean Anderson was making a vertical incision in the patient's lower abdomen.

Not good.

It meant they weren't worried about scarring or anything except getting that baby out as quickly as possible.

He moved into position. "Baby's obs?"

Sean glanced his way for a second, but didn't slow his pace. "Heart rate is good, but there was no time to administer anything to speed maturation of the lungs. I don't know what we're going to find."

He nodded, but knew better than to say anything else. They were in a fight for the life of the mother. Saving both mum and child was always the goal. All he could do was his best once the baby was born.

Sean opened the uterus and reached inside. Out came a perfectly formed baby boy. So tiny. So damned tiny.

His heart seized as they clamped and cut the cord, not even trying to get the baby to breathe.

"She's bleeding. I need some suction in here!" Sean handed the preemie off to him, caught up in the struggle to get the mum's bleeding under control. Eclampsia's high blood pressure put the patient at risk for heart attack or stroke. When medication didn't work, the only solution was to remove what was causing the spike in pressure: the baby.

The nurses assigned to the infant rushed with him to the table, everyone having his own job. They suctioned the mouth, administered oxygen, rubbed the baby with towels…anything to get him breathing. Nothing. Listening to the baby's heart, he found the rate slow. Too slow. "We need to intubate, right now."

There were two battles being fought in the room. One to save the life of the mother. And one to save the life of her baby.

In the background, he vaguely heard Sean still yelling out orders to those on his team. His own team of nurses worked with a timed precision that made him proud on one level. On another, he wondered if it would be enough.

Once the intubation tube was in place and oxygen was pumped directly into the lungs, he waited until another nurse had the feed electrodes pasted to the baby boy's chest. They turned on the monitor. The straight line turned to spikes. But they were shallow. And still too slow. Only ninety beats per minute when it should have been at least a hundred and twenty.

A quick test of reflexes found the baby did indeed have

them. But for how long? At just over six months, it was iffy as to whether the baby would even survive the night. But he was determined to give the infant the best possible chance. "Let's get him over to SCBU and see about those lungs."

The baby was just over twenty-four weeks and weighed in at only one pound two ounces. Twenty-five was the normal threshold for viability, but, as rare as it was, he'd seen babies this premature make it.

He glanced back at Sean. They were suturing the mother. Their eyes met. "How's the baby?"

"I won't know for a while. Mum?"

"The bleeding's under control. Blood pressure is coming down already. I think we've rounded the corner."

That might be true for Sean's patient, but for his own tiny charge that corner was still far in the distance. He could only hope the baby held on long enough for them to reach it.

"My parents left yesterday."

Pulling into the driveway of Dean's friend's house, Jess could already see several horses out in a nearby pasture, while another one stood at the fence line next to the car just to their right. Heavy vapor poured from its nostrils with every puff of air, making the creature look like a dragon from a fairy tale. He might as well be breathing fire, from where Jess sat.

"I don't think this is a good idea." In fact, Jess was sure it was a very bad idea. As was the brilliant one to go ice skating after this was all over.

Assuming she survived the first ordeal.

Her white skates from her teenage years were tucked into the boot of Dean's expensive car, along with his own black ones. Somehow she couldn't see him twirling around at an ice rink. He just looked too broad. Too strong.

Okay, so she would live. She had to, because that was definitely one picture she wanted to see. Of Dean weaving to and fro, making patterns in the ice.

"You're going to do fine."

Right. That was easy for him to say. "Just look at that one. He seems ready to take down anyone who ventures too close."

Dean glanced over at where she was pointing and laughed. "That's Thor."

"Thor?" Her head jerked around again to look at the pure white horse. She noticed no one else was around him. In fact, another fence stood between this horse and the rest of the herd in the distance. "Are you serious? That's his name?"

Dean nodded. "Yep. Because he swings a pretty serious hammer."

She closed her eyes to shut out the twin plumes of steam that were still emerging with the beast's every breath. "Oh, God. I don't even want to know what that means. Has he kicked anyone *recently*?"

"Kicked?" His head cocked to the side. Then he smiled again. "No. And you probably *don't* want to know why he's called that. Let's just say his mares haven't lodged any complaints."

Heat flashed up her face, along with relief. "Oh. So he's not mean."

"Not at all. For a stallion, he's pretty much a pussycat."

Somehow, she wasn't seeing it. She scrunched further down into her winter parka, hoping the dark fabric proved true to its promise that it could go from earthy to elegant without a hitch. Because right now, this was about as earthy as she could imagine getting.

"Let's go say hello," he continued.

"Oh. I'm fine. I'm sure he won't think me rude if I just sit this one out."

He gave her another grin. "It's a perfect photo op. We can shoot one of you standing next to him."

"Next to…?" Her eyes widened. "Oh, no, I don't think so."

"You'll have to shed your coat, of course. The pasture is still green enough to pretend it's autumn, if that's what one is expecting to see."

He acted as if he hadn't heard her at all. "I said, I don't think so."

Tweaking her nose, he popped open the door and exited his vehicle. "It's okay. I promise."

He came around and held open the door for her. Unfortunately, the day wasn't as chilly as it could be. In fact, it felt more like a typical autumn day than mid-December. So much for her hope to be snowed out. There wasn't even a damned cloud in the sky.

Let's get this over with.

When she got out and stood next to Dean, he fingered her hair for a minute, startling her. She jerked her head to look at him, but he just shrugged. "Just thinking it was a good thing you didn't wear a hair clip."

Did the animal bite? There were still a good couple of meters between her and Thor. "How about I stand here and you get a quick shot?"

Just then someone came out of the house. Dean smiled and crossed over to the man, who had to be pushing fifty, shaking his hand.

"Good to see you both." He glanced at Jess. "Is this her?"

"It is indeed. Jess, this is Clifton Mathers. Cliff, my friend Jess Black."

His friend. At least he wasn't introducing her as his girlfriend. But why would he?

"Nothing to be afraid of, missy. Dean told me to make sure to give you one of our mildest mounts."

"As mild as Thor?" The words just came out of nowhere.

Cliff shook his head. "No, I've got a little bitty thing picked out for you. One of our ponies."

"A— A pony?" All she could think of was the beast who'd tossed her over its shoulder as if she were nothing more than a hunk of fairy floss years ago.

"She's a tall pony. You'll suit her just fine."

Great. The combination of pony and tall did not make her feel any better.

Dean nodded at the fence. "I thought we might get a shot of us with Thor."

She'd so hoped he'd forgotten about doing that.

"I think Thor would be delighted," Cliff said.

Delighted. Well, at least one of them would be.

Dean waited until she shed her jacket, then handed his phone to Cliff. He eyed her when she made no move to walk over to the fence. Did he think she was just going to skip over there and hug the animal? Not bloody likely.

Unwilling to look like a total fool, she finally allowed herself to be tugged toward the white horizontal slats that made up the fence line. If she'd hoped Dean would keep his body in between her and the horse, she was soon disabused of that notion when he let go of her and moved to the other side.

What had she been thinking?

What had started as a quick fabrication by Dean to get her sister off her back had turned into a huge production that now included her parents.

Why did Dean even care what her sister thought?

Worse, he'd warned her that Abbie had talked to a couple of the nurses.

That made her swallow. She did not want to go down as a tick mark on a list of this man's known conquests. She'd already had that happen once with Martin. Theirs had been a whirlwind affair and engagement. But once he'd met Abbie, that had been it. He had no longer been interested in her.

"Love, you need to scoot in a bit closer so I can get all of you in the picture."

Cliff was speaking to her.

Closer? She gulped and peeked to the side. There was scarcely a meter between her and the horse as it was. She plucked up a few more ounces of courage and then side-stepped twice. A warm current of air gusted across her neck.

Ugh! The animal's breath—not to mention she was probably within reach of those huge white teeth now. "Could we do this quickly?"

Dean reached over and took her hand, giving it a reassuring squeeze. It almost worked.

Then, something warm and rubbery touched her neck, just above the collar of her light sweater, and brushed across it. She froze, waiting for a set of equine chompers to latch onto her. But they didn't. A curious snuffling sound met her ears.

She chuckled. She couldn't help it. The animal's lips tickled. And he certainly didn't seem to want to hurt her.

A few of her muscles relaxed, and she glanced sideways to find one of the horse's deep brown eyes fastened on her. And the expression in them seemed...kind.

She and the horse continued to stare at each other, his neck curved in her direction, grassy breath sliding across her cheek with every breath he took. A sense of awe filled her.

"Wow." It was the only word that came to mind.

"Perfect." Cliff's voice broke the spell, and she blinked back to herself. "I got some great shots."

He had? When?

Dean came around the front of the horse and nudged the animal's head away from her. "See? Not so bad." His murmured words came right before he dropped a quick kiss on her mouth.

He pulled back almost immediately, but it was too late. Her lips tingled and a strange twitchy sensation came to life in her belly muscles.

Boneless.

That was what she felt. She stiffened her knees and forced them to hold her upright. It was just a quick friendly kiss of reassurance, like that hand squeeze had been a few minutes ago.

Except she could almost guarantee that friends didn't make each other feel like that. As if she wanted him to linger and reassure her some more.

She'd even forgotten about Thor's presence beside her—although he was back to snuffling around her sweater, his horsey lips blubbering and vibrating almost as much as her legs.

Thor's antics had put her so at ease that when it actually came time to sit on a pony's back—and Cliff was right, this particular pony was taller than the one from her childhood—it was all anticlimactic and dull. They got their pictures with no incidents and the next thing she knew they were back in his car and driving to the ice-skating arena.

Dean handed over his phone and told her to scroll through the pictures, to see if there were any good ones.

In the first few shots, even Jess could read the fear on

her face, but as she continued scrolling she saw a change take place. At around the twentieth photo, she swallowed. Cliff had captured the moment Dean's lips met hers. The angle was perfect, showing that her eyes were closed and that she seemed to be leaning into that brief touch.

Damn. If she could see that, then…

Maybe she could figure out how to delete it before Dean came across it on his own. But just as her finger hovered over the screen his hand came over hers, stopping it. "If you're doing what I think you are, don't. I did that for the benefit of your parents."

Horror washed over her. The kiss had been staged?

How could she be so stupid? She'd actually believed…

With lightning speed she ran through the rest of the pictures without really seeing them and then handed the phone back. As if he realized something was wrong, he touched her cheek. "Hey. Just because it was planned, doesn't mean I didn't enjoy it."

Far from reassuring her, it only made her feel worse. He had no problem kissing her and enjoying the physical pleasure without ever letting that pleasure seep any deeper. But as their failed bet had proved, she wasn't nearly as adept at keeping things light and easy as he was.

If she was going to survive the next couple of weeks, though, she was going to have to figure out how Dean managed it. And then she needed to copy him step for step.

Otherwise, this man could very well break her heart.

CHAPTER EIGHT

JESS'S SKATES SCRAPED across the ice, bringing her to a halt right in front of him. She hadn't said anything about being an expert skater. But she was. And the healthy pink flush to her cheeks was a welcome sight after the pale translucence her skin had had in those first few days that her niece had been in the SCBU.

"Having fun?" he asked. He had to admit that he was. In spite of the news of his father's release from prison, and his concern about the preemie of their eclampsia patient, Dean was having a good time.

And most of it was due to the woman in front of him. This was why he didn't do relationships. He'd learned the hard way that if you got too attached to a person, they would go away. His dad had gone to prison for beating his mother—which was a good thing—but it was damned hard to obliterate your feelings for a parent, no matter how heinous his behavior might be.

And then his mum. As soon as she'd recovered from that last beating, she'd decided she'd had enough of the whole ugly scene. Dean had been sixteen. Legally old enough to be emancipated, if they'd gone before a magistrate. But had his mum done that? No. She'd simply cut him loose and left him behind saying he was old enough to be on his own. After all, he'd already been working and had been almost through school.

And yet he still loved his mother, even after all these years, even if he hated the choices she'd made along the way.

"I'm having a wonderful time," Jess said. "At least skating is one thing I'm not afraid of."

"We should take some pictures here as well. After all, that's why we came, isn't it?"

A shadow fell across her face, the first since they'd put their skates on a half-hour ago. Jess was head and shoulders above him as far as skill levels went. But that didn't mean he hadn't liked watching her skim across the ice like some kind of professional athlete. He'd even seen a few of the men on the ice watch her as she flew past.

She wasn't going to pick anyone up here, though. Even though their bet was over and done with, he wrapped an arm around her waist and reeled her in. Jess gave a quiet squeak. "What are you doing?"

He leaned in close. "Making sure everyone knows that you're mine for the day."

But not for the night. Which brought him back to that failed bet. Worst decision in history. He should have offered himself up for her little experiment at the very beginning, and been done with it. No more suppressed instincts. No more wondering what it might have been like if they'd fallen into bed together.

He was an expert at keeping his emotions out of any sexual encounters. He couldn't say the same of Jess, which was what had ultimately stopped him. One of his biggest rules had always been to make sure the woman knew where things stood and what she could expect once the night was over.

There were women out there who could do that—

despite what Jess thought. He'd met them. Slept with them. And everyone was still friends. Well, maybe not friends, but they could exchange a friendly smile and a few words of greeting if they happened across each other later.

Yep, it would be different with Jess.

As if she sensed his thoughts she pulled back, throwing him a quick smile. "I'm actually not anyone's. For the day, or otherwise."

With that, she whisked past him, doing an expert spin and then settling in to skate with easy grace, hands behind her back, eyes half closed as if soaking in everything she could.

He found himself doing the same. And since he was still standing in the same spot he'd been a few minutes ago, he forced himself to move, feeling like a lumbering oaf compared to Jess's lithe movements.

She passed him again with an amused wave. A flicker of irritation went through him, this time. Maybe they should have stayed at Cliff's house and settled in for a visit. But he'd wanted to do something that Jess would find fun, rather than stressful. The pictures had just been an excuse.

Instead, it was Dean who was stressed. Other couples held hands and moseyed around the rink and a small group of men stood on the outside perimeter watching the skaters—a few of them, the ones who'd eyed Jess earlier, probably wondering if she was single. Well, hopefully they'd gotten the message when he'd put his arm around her.

Jess, however, didn't seem to care if anyone was ogling her from the sidelines. Well, then, he would just force himself not to care either.

"Helloooo…"

She was back, this time turning around and skating backward so that she faced him. "I just thought of something. If you're in a hurry to get back, we can take a few pictures and leave. I know this wasn't supposed to be a real outing, just a photo op."

"I'm fine. I haven't been away from the hospital in ages, other than to go home to sleep. It feels good to be out in the real world." Something came to him. "But we do need some pictures. Better to do it now while there's still plenty of light and people."

He took her hand and pulled her toward the railing across from them, heading straight toward one of the men who'd been staring at her. With an easy smile he held up his phone. "Would you mind shooting a few shots of us as we go around the rink?"

The way the man's face fell would have been comical, if he hadn't been so obvious about his stares. The rental skates on the ground beside him said that he might even have gone out onto the ice in an attempt to reel in his catch once he'd singled one of them out. Wasn't that what Dean would have done?

Possibly. Hopefully he wouldn't have been quite so cold-blooded about the whole thing. It was one thing to engage in conversation that led to something else. It was another thing entirely to sit there like a predator, hoping to find a likely target.

Something inside of him whispered a protest. Was he certain he wasn't like that?

Yes. Definitely.

"Sure thing, buddy." The man's accent marked him as American. "Just let me know how it works."

How it works is this: you stand there and take pictures and leave Jess the hell alone.

Dean showed him how to operate the camera function, hoping that the man didn't just take off with it. Again, he had the idea that the bloke was just hoping to score a little something extra while on holiday. Well, he'd have to look elsewhere.

"Thanks." He tossed the American one final glance before taking to the ice with Jess in tow. Soon, she turned the tables, however, pulling him along at a speed that was a bit faster than he was used to.

"Don't forget you have an amateur on your hands."

"That's hard for me to believe. I think you're an expert."

In other things, was her inference. His irritation spiked a bit higher. It was one thing to have had that chat and bet about casual sex, it was another thing entirely to have her act as if it were a communicable disease that she had no intention of catching. Did she really think she was immune?

He moved behind her and wrapped his arms around her waist, his skates moving to the outside of hers and coasting. "Wh-what are you doing?"

"The man's taking pictures, remember?"

"Pictures. Right."

He leaned in and nuzzled her neck, feeling like old Thor and seeing exactly why the horse had engaged in a little love talk of his own. She smelled wonderful. And her skin was soft. Silky...

Someone sliced past, throwing them a quick glare. It was then that Dean realized the coasting had slowed to a crawl and that they were almost standing still, people flowing around them.

He ignored them. Pictures. He wanted her father to buy into their story.

The problem was, Dean was starting to buy into it himself. He kissed her ear. Her cheek. Slowly moving along it until he reached the corner of her mouth. Suddenly Jess spun around on one skate. But not to get away. No. She was now facing him. Looking up at him as if she wanted nothing more than for him to...

And so he did. He touched his mouth to hers, glorying in the chill that clung to her lips, the scent and taste of the hot cocoa she'd drunk before coming out on the ice. The combination surrounded his senses.

He gripped the edges of her parka and drew her closer. Using her skill on the ice to hold himself up. At least that was what he told himself. In reality, he just wanted her against him. Wanted to slide his hands beneath all of those clothes and feel the warm skin of her stomach... her breasts.

That was what finally pulled him from his trance. He'd done this to prove she wasn't entirely immune. Well, hell, it seemed he was the one who'd caught something. And he'd better figure out a cure and quick.

He drew back. "I think he's probably gotten enough."

Jess gasped, looking as if he'd just slapped her. And rightly so. It was the second time he'd pretended a kiss was all about the pictures, when in reality it was all about her. About the way she made him feel. But if she thought he was the king of casual sex, now was the time to play the part.

"I'm sure he has." Her eyes turned frosty. "Time to go see, isn't it? Actually it's past time. And I think I'm ready to call it a day, if you don't mind. If you'll send me copies of the pictures, I'll forward them to my parents. And that'll be that. Thank you for bailing me out, but you're now off the hook."

He didn't want her to just run back to her rabbit hole and disappear, as much as he knew that was exactly what should happen. For his own peace of mind.

"If I remember right, I put myself on that hook, not you." Well, that made no sense at all, but it was the only thing he could think of.

Dean let go of her jacket and took what he hoped was a casual step back, only to have his skates suddenly shoot out from under him, landing him straight on his ass.

CHAPTER NINE

"I HAVE TO go home."

Abbie stood over her baby's cot, gripping some kind of small bottle.

"What do you mean you have to go home? What about Marissa?"

"Mum rang me this morning. Jerry is in hospital. He has pneumonia."

Jess's heart dropped. Her four-year-old nephew. "Oh, God, I'm sorry. What about Martin?"

Her twin's head turned in her direction for a second, but there was no accusation in her eyes for once. "He'll come with me, of course, and then it's back to work for him tomorrow."

"Already?"

Abbie nodded. "He cut short a business trip to come to Cambridge. There are some things he needs to tie up before he can officially go on paternity leave. He didn't expect the baby to…arrive when she did."

Guilt surrounded Jess once again. "I'm so sorry for what happened."

"I think I'm being punished." The words were spoken with a quiet resignation that gave Jess pause.

Her sister had been quick enough to blame her for this last week. What had changed?

"Why would you say something like that?"

"Two of my children are now sick." She shifted the bottle from one hand to the other. Jess tilted her head and peered at it a bit closer.

Concealer.

Was she putting on makeup here in the SCBU? When she moved her glance back to her sister's face, all that met her were dark circles and mussed hair. Her sister was always so sure of herself. So careful about her appearance.

Something seemed off.

Well, she had two children in hospital. Any mother would be frantic—feeling torn between the two of them, whether to stay or whether to go.

Jess laid her hand on the top of the special-care cot. "You're not being punished. And I'll keep an eye on her, Abbie. If anything at all comes up, I'll ring you immediately."

"Every day. Please ring me every day."

One of the other babies cried and a nurse came in to check on him before Jess could move. "I will. She's so very precious, isn't she?"

She looked down at the tiny human, eyes tracing over the rise and fall of her chest. The kick of a little leg. The one that had…

The birthmark. It was gone. Jess leaned a little closer.

No. It wasn't gone. That was what the concealer was for. All traces of compassion rushed away like a torrent. "You put makeup on her leg? What is wrong with you, Abbie?"

Abbie dropped into the chair and covered her face with her hands. The other nurse finished what she was doing and then retreated to the far corner, probably wanting no part of what was likely to be a drama of the first order. It always seemed to be, where her sister was concerned.

"I…" Abbie tilted her head back to look at her, and

Jess was shocked to see tears. "You have no idea what I've done."

Were they still talking about the concealer? Her sister had mentioned being punished. Did she think the birthmark was part of that?

"What is it, then?" And where in the world was Martin? Shouldn't he be here with his wife, if they were leaving?

She handed the bottle to Jess. "It's not what you think. I don't want the baby to pay for what I did."

"You didn't do anything. And you can't cover up her birthmark. It's just a tiny spot. I don't understand why it's such a big deal."

Her sister sighed. "Martin works so much. It seems like he's always off on some business trip. I used to wonder if he was coming to see you."

"Of course he wasn't. I would never do that to you. Or to anyone." Something churned in her stomach, and she wasn't sure she really wanted to hear any more.

Abbie's mouth tightened. "You always were the perfect one."

"Please don't."

"I'm sorry." She stood up and seemed to pull herself back together. "Martin is packing my things now, and we leave in two hours. You'll ring me?"

"Of course." She handed the bottle back to Abbie. "I know you're not asking me to put this on her."

"No. It was just stupidity on my part." She curled her fingers around the concealer, knuckles showing white. "I'll let you know when we arrive in London."

"And please let me know how Jerry is. Give him a gentle hug from his Aunt Jess."

She needed to make more of an effort to visit her nephews. Even if she and Abbie didn't always get along, the boys shouldn't have to pay the price.

"I will." Abbie unexpectedly wrapped her in a tight hug. "I'm sorry. For everything. I hope someday you'll understand."

At the moment, Jess didn't understand anything, except that her sister was hurting and for the first time was letting her share that burden just a little. Feeling a little weepy and out of sorts herself after what had happened with Dean on the ice two days ago, she put her arms around her sister and squeezed her right back.

There was hope. There had to be. For Abbie. And for her.

Isabel Delamere was posting a flier of some type on the staff board. An Australian obstetrician who'd been seconded to Cambridge Royal Hospital, Isabel had quickly become a part of daily life in the maternity unit.

Dean moved in to take a closer look at the paper. Something about a staff Christmas party. His brows went up. "Haven't we had a couple of those already?"

She smiled at him. "A couple. But one was for prospective adoptive parents in Aaron Cartwright's program. Hope Sanders and Bonnie Reid helped organise it. But we haven't had anything for just the staff yet. A few people felt we needed a more adult type of party."

When Dean's brows crept even higher, she laughed. "Not that kind of party. Just a fancy venue with pretty frocks, flashy tuxes and lots of festivity." A shadow passed across her face. "Some of us could really use that right about now."

She was right. He'd been tense for the last couple of days, ever since that kiss with Jess at the ice-skating arena. He'd spent that night in bed, his imagination exploding at what might have happened had he just kept his mouth shut.

As a result he'd become more and more irritable. And

frustrated. He'd found himself in the strange position of lusting after someone he shouldn't have.

He knew it would be the worst kind of mistake. But that didn't stop his head from picturing it, in explicit detail.

Speak of the devil. Here she came. Head down as if she were going to power past him without a glance. Except that Isabel called out to her, waving her over.

And over she came. Shoulders hunched. Arms stiff at her sides. As if heading to an execution.

Isabel nodded at the poster. "We're quite late getting this under way, but were hoping you could help spread the word." The other woman touched her arm. "And maybe even get us a head count? You'll be there, right?"

Looking at the writing and the bright image of a huge fancy Christmas tree, Jess drew in a quick breath. "It's at the Sarasota?"

"Yes, super posh, so wear something fancy." Isabel waved a sheaf of papers. "Well, I have more of these to get up. If you could let me know how many you think can make it, that would be fab. I expect to see you there." With that, she was off on her next mission.

Dean studied Jess's face. It was as if she couldn't stop staring at the poster. "What is it?"

"That's where my parents had their anniversary party." Light brown eyes closed, and she swallowed. "I'll never be able to forget that night. Or what happened."

Moving closer, he looped an arm around her shoulders. "I'm sorry."

"I can't go. I know it'll disappoint Isabel, but—"

"I think you should go."

"What?"

"Face it head-on. Replace bad memories with something more pleasant. Otherwise, every time you hear the hotel's name, you'll associate it with what happened."

If anyone knew that, it was him. Just like the tonic water he'd forced himself to down at Jess's place. It had ended up being a good thing, the newer memory supplanting some of the ones from his past. Maybe Jess could do the same thing. Replace a bad memory with a not so bad memory. "I'll go with you, if it'll help."

When storm clouds formed in her eyes, he shook his head. "Not for a photo op, but as a friend. If you get there and realize you can't handle being there, we'll leave." He stepped in front of her and tilted her chin. "No one should have to face something like this alone. Not if you don't have to."

The air seemed to crackle between them for several seconds, and then she drew a big breath. Nodded. "Thank you. I think I'll take you up on it." She paused. "If you're sure?"

Letting go of her, he took a step back, afraid he might be tempted to lean closer and capture that satiny mouth with his.

"Very sure." Maybe this would help ease the tension between them and drop them back on safer ground. He grinned, a sense of relief flowing through him. "I haven't worn a tuxedo in ages. This gives me a good excuse to put on something besides a lab coat or scrubs."

Jess glanced down at her own blue medical garb and smiled up at him. "It will be fun to let my hair down for a while."

Her blonde hair was pulled back in its customary ponytail, that gray streak looking like an exclamation point that had been tipped on its side. Bold. Unapologetic. She could have dyed it to go with the rest of her hair, and yet she let it run free—like an inner wild child who refused to be tamed or subdued.

He liked it. Glad that she'd left it natural. He took his thumb and ran it over the narrow strip of hair until he got to the elastic in back. "Isabel said the party would do everyone some good. She might be right."

Before he could even think about what he was doing, he touched her cheek and continued, "Don't worry, we'll make sure Marissa is well cared for while we're there."

She bit her lip. "That reminds me. Abbie is going home. One of her other children is ill." He listened without speaking as Jess filled him in on what was happening in short choppy phrases.

"She did what?" He couldn't help but interrupt when she mentioned her sister had put makeup on the baby. "Why would she? There's always a danger of contamination."

"I know. And she acted oddly once I'd realized what she'd done. Like she wanted to tell me something, but changed her mind."

"What do you think it was?"

"I have no idea. But I have a feeling it has to do with Martin."

At that, Dean frowned. Surely Abbie wasn't accusing her sister of going after him again. "How so?"

Reaching back, she tightened her ponytail. "She talked about him working so much. I think she suspects he's having an affair. But then she talked about the problems with Marissa being a punishment for something. Something *she'd* done."

"If she thinks Martin is the one having the affair…" Another staff member murmured an apology as they went to move past them to look at the flier. Dean eased Jess over to the side.

"Maybe she feels like she drove him away somehow." Jess glanced toward the ceiling. "I have no idea. I told her I'd look after Marissa until she gets back. She's written up a power of attorney so that I can make medical decisions for the baby, if something terrible happens. I just hope I don't have to. I want her to grow and thrive."

"It's what we all want. For each and every one of those babies."

Including the preemie from the eclampsia case. So far the baby was hanging in there, despite the odds.

"You're incredibly good at what you do." Jess's soft voice held a sincerity that made him swallow.

"Thank you. We all do our best."

"No. I think it's more than that. You have a drive that I don't see in every doctor. Yes, they care about their patients, but there's something different about the way you go about it."

Too close. He didn't want her looking inside and seeing his own shattered childhood. Or realizing how scared and alone he'd felt during his years at home. As devastated as he'd been by his mother's abandonment, in a way it had come as a relief. He'd become self-reliant. No longer depending on anyone other than himself.

Staring at the one woman who might be able to see beneath his flirty, carefree mask, he forced himself to push it on a little tighter. "I'm just doing what I was trained to do. Helping my patients get the very best medical care available. Nothing more. Nothing less."

Less. Now there was a good word. One that was beginning to sound better and better.

As in seeing less of Jess.

And as soon as that Christmas party was over, he was going to retreat to his own little self-reliant corner, and this time he would make sure he stayed there.

CHAPTER TEN

"You two look adorable together. You have no idea how long your father and I have waited for this."

Her mum's voice made tears spring to her eyes. Staring at the upper right-hand corner of her computer where a slideshow of the shots she'd sent were blinking past one after the other, she had to admit, it all looked far too real.

The pictures of them beside Thor had a spontaneity that she certainly hadn't felt when she'd been standing there. But her face was pink, her teeth digging into her lower lip, while Dean's eyes held a mischievous glow that transported her back to that day. He'd just finished telling her where the horse's name had come from. And Cliff had caught the moment perfectly.

And the ice skating. Dean had handed his phone over to that stranger and they'd staged another scene. This one had him standing behind her, arms wrapped around her waist. Jess's head was tilted back so that she leaned against his shoulder. If she closed her eyes, she could almost smell that earthy, manly scent that had drifted past her nose as she'd stood within the circle of his arms.

She'd wanted him in that moment. Desperately. The fact that she would just be one more woman on an ever-growing list hadn't seemed to matter. It was getting harder and harder to convince her body that sleeping with him would be a big mistake. Especially now, when she couldn't quite remember why that was.

"Well, don't marry us off just yet." What else could she say? They weren't getting married. Ever. And there really wasn't a need to keep pretending. Abbie had already left and so had Martin.

But they had to come back to get the baby, didn't they?

"Even I can read the writing on the wall." Her father's smile came through the video chat. They'd convinced him, evidently.

Unfortunately, she'd almost convinced herself as well, which would be a royal disaster. She did not need to get caught up in the fairy tale Dean had spun for her family. If she did, she might never be able to free herself again.

An image of Dean crouched in the corner of an enormous web, waiting to devour her, came to mind.

Only when he climbed toward her—making his way along the sticky fibers of the trap he'd spun—he didn't have the menace of a spider...but that of a lover. The same man who'd held her on that ice, his strong arms binding her to him. What if sleeping with him set her free from that web? Because what was really holding her there were all of those *what-would-it-be-like?* thoughts that kept going through her mind.

Like the ones filling her mind right now.

No. Can't happen.

He only wanted to satisfy his physical needs.

And she didn't?

Hmm...maybe putting a stop to his advances at the pub hadn't been such a smart idea, after all. What better person to teach her about casual sex than the king of casual sex: Dean Edwards?

What would be so terrible about that, really, if they both knew where things stood?

That wasn't what she'd thought all those nights ago.

She shook her head to clear it, realizing her parents were still staring at her.

The writing. Her dad had said he could see the writing on the wall.

"We're not going to rush into anything. We're both busy people."

"Not too busy to get married and have a family, surely?" her mum protested.

She had a point as far as that was concerned. Jess didn't make much time for her personal life. Ever since she and Martin had broken things off, she hadn't wanted to date or do anything else for that matter. Which was why she allowed herself to be talked into working extra shifts. She was so knackered on most nights she went home and fell right into bed—alone.

And forty years from now, would she be settled into the same routine? Or maybe she'd have ninety-nine cats to keep her warm in bed.

Dean had been so sweet after her reaction to the Christmas party's venue. He could have easily found a date for the evening. Instead, he'd offered to go with her and leave whenever she'd had enough. He'd put her feelings ahead of his own.

Would he be as attentive in bed?

Jess shivered. She had no doubt he would be an excellent lover. How else would he have gotten the reputation he had? If he were a jerk about things afterward, surely she would have heard about it? But no. Women swooned over him.

"We're trying to play things by ear, Mum. These things can't be hurried."

Her mother made a scoffing sound. "Your sister has

quite a head start on you in the department of providing us with grandchildren."

Jess tensed. "You're getting way ahead of yourself."

Maybe her mother sensed something in her voice, because she came back with, "Of course I am. But speaking of children, how is my newest little granddaughter?"

"She's doing wonderfully. We're going to try to give her her first bottle this afternoon."

"Abbie will be so pleased to hear it."

Her father had gone silent in the background, but he was looking at her through the computer with a slight frown on his face, even as the pictures of her and Dean kept flashing by in another window of the screen.

Oh, no. She knew that expression. He was about to ask something tricky.

She tried to head things off at the pass. "How is Jerry doing? Is he still in hospital?"

"He is. He's quite ill, actually." Her mum waved her hand in front of the screen when Jess's eyes widened. "His life isn't in danger, of course, but you can just tell he's poorly. Abbie did the right thing in coming home."

"It couldn't have been an easy decision." Her sister's behavior that last day still puzzled her. The whole putting makeup on the baby's leg and then those enigmatic words about being punished. But at least she finally seemed ready to make peace with their own personal past.

"It wasn't. All she talks about is going back for the baby once Jerry is well enough."

"Marissa will be here for a couple more weeks, I should think. She still has a bit of weight to put on."

"Jess." Her father's voice pulled at her. "Are you happy?"

The question was so far removed from what they'd been talking about that it took her brain a moment or two to untangle the words. Once she did, they hit her between the eyes. She squirmed in her seat, hating that she was deceiving them like this. She should have just taken whatever Abbie dished out…except that Abbie was making not only herself miserable, but everyone around her. Going along with Dean's fib had seemed a small price to pay at the time. But it had grown into this gargantuan monster that required more lies to keep the original one from being discovered.

"He's a good man." Words very much like the ones she'd said as she'd stood in front of that poster for the Christmas party. And it was true. Dean had been a good sport. It didn't hurt that he was also a great kisser. The memory of his lips moving across hers in front of her house came to mind. And then at the pub. On the ice.

She wanted to kiss him again. Wanted to find some measure of satisfaction in his arms.

Should she? He'd offered to leave the Christmas party early if she wanted to. What if she asked him to leave for a completely different reason?

Would he say yes?

After what she'd done at the pub? She had no idea.

"I didn't ask that." Her dad wasn't going to let this alone evidently. "I asked if you were happy."

Yes. She was. This time with Dean had brought her joy. He was fun, sexy, brave. And watching him cradle Marissa in those big hands had done a number on her heart. She was happy to have spent this time with him. Even if it never went any further.

"Yes. I'm happy. Does that satisfy you?"

Her mum sighed. "I can just see the love in your eyes when you say that."

She could? Then Jess had better smack it right back out of there. She didn't love him.

Like him? Yes. Lust after him? Um, double yes.

That was what she'd been doing just moments ago. Lusting. Was she going to do something about it?

Maybe. For one night of hot sex.

Warmth swept along her inner thighs, setting areas to tingling that needed to remain still and quiet. She was on the phone with her parents, for goodness' sake.

"I'm sure Dean will be thrilled to hear you say that." She didn't roll her eyes. At least not outwardly. But inside? Oh, yes, they were rolling all around like those fake glasses with the googly eyes.

Suddenly superstitious about everything that had happened, she crossed her fingers behind her back and hoped the universe took pity on her situation. The last thing she needed was for it to look down at her and decide to give her exactly what she deserved.

"Well, I'd probably better go. I need to go shopping for a dress for the Christmas party and I have a shift in the morning."

"Christmas party?" Her mum's brows went up. "This is the first I've heard of this."

"It's for the hospital staff. They're having it at the same hotel as your anniversary party, actually."

"Such a beautiful place. Are you going with Dean?"

Finally. One thing she was not going to have to lie about. "I am."

"Well, we definitely wouldn't want to keep you from shopping. Pick out something that will knock him dead."

"Not too dead," her dad interjected with a smile. "We want him alive and well." His voice turned serious. "After that business with Martin, I'm glad you've found someone."

Her heart ached all over again. Her dad had never quite forgiven her ex for breaking off their engagement, although he hid it well. But Jess saw glimpses of it every once in a while. Just a flash of narrowed eyes or a frown when he listened to his son-in-law, but she'd caught it, just the same.

"Dean's a peach, all right." She forced a bright smile. "I've got to run, though. Chat again soon?"

"After the party, if not before." Her mum planted a kiss on her husband's cheek. "We'll want to hear every detail."

If Jess got the nerve up to do what she was thinking of doing, there would be at least one part of the evening her parents would never hear about.

Because she *had* made up her mind—at least she hoped so. She just needed to drum up the courage to follow through.

She was going to back Dean into a corner at that very posh hotel and ask him to spend the night with her. She did want a fling. A real one. Not with just anyone—and certainly not with some stranger from the pub—but with Dean. Maybe then she could stop obsessing about the man.

He did casual sex on a regular basis, so there'd be no chance of him getting the wrong idea about where they were headed afterward. Right?

So it was settled. She would do it.

And then she'd just hope and pray he didn't do what she'd done at that pub...and turn around and walk away.

She was feeding the baby.

Dean stood back against the wall and watched with interest, a lump forming in his throat. Jess didn't know he was here—not yet, anyway—he'd seen her through the window and quietly entered the SCBU through the side door. All her attention had been on the tiny infant cradled in her arms, cooing and talking softly to her. "Good girl.

Mummy is going to be so happy to know you're drinking from your bottle."

A few of the tubes had been removed this morning, once they knew for sure that the baby's suck reflex was going strong. Using a gloved pinkie finger, Dean had been thrilled when the infant's head had tracked the path of his finger, trying to root around and latch on. The next step had been to introduce the real thing.

And the baby had done it. She'd latched onto the bottle's teat and started sucking with enthusiasm.

That wasn't the only good news. The baby born to the woman with eclampsia was also improving in small steady increments. In fact, that baby was in the cot right next to Marissa's. Dean had come to check on him.

Jess murmured again and the knot in his throat tightened further. She was going to make such a good mother. Unlike his own, who'd been so young that she hadn't known her own mind. Or how to protect herself—and Dean—from the drunken fool she'd married.

He hadn't heard anything else about his father since he'd received the news that he'd been let out of prison. The one good thing was that his mum was long gone. He'd never be able to hurt her again. And Dean would make sure the man didn't get close enough to anyone he cared about to hurt them either.

Exactly who would that be? Dean had no one. And that was how he wanted to keep it.

His gaze traveled back to Jess, and he realized her light brown eyes were no longer focused on the baby. She was staring right at him, a question written in her gaze.

"What?" he mouthed.

She shook her head.

Quietly moving over to where she sat, he crouched down beside her. "How's she doing?"

Jess smiled. The sight almost knocked him over. There was a radiance to her eyes and a soul-searing happiness in the softness of her face that spoke of a woman in love.

He swallowed. No one had ever looked at him like that.

And even though he knew the expression was for the minute creature she held in her arms, he could pretend for just a few seconds what it might be like to have had a mum like this one.

Only Jess wasn't a mum. And this wasn't her child.

He shook himself back to reality.

"Brilliantly," Jess murmured. "Just look at her."

In order to stop staring at the woman, he did as she asked and glanced down at the baby. With a tiny tuft of light hair on her head and blue eyes that fixed on Jess's face, she sucked with quiet enthusiasm. A drop of white appeared at the outer corner of her lips and he reached for Jess's arm where the burping rag had slipped and used it to carefully dab at the speck.

On impulse, he leaned over and kissed the baby's head, smiling when she shifted as if irritated by the interruption. When his attention moved back to Jess, he was surprised to find her eyes moist.

"Are you okay?"

"Just happy that she's getting stronger."

"We all are."

She pulled in a deep breath. "Yes. Of course. So did you get yourself a tux? The party is just days away."

"I already have one."

Her lips tightened slightly. "I imagine you go to quite a few fancy parties."

"Not so many, no. I bought the tux for a friend's wedding before I realized that most people simply rent and return them. I figured since I had it, I could use it whenever

I needed one for a fancy dinner." His brows lifted. "Don't think I've used it twice since then, actually."

"Oh." The tense lines beside her mouth eased. "Well, I bought a new dress and a killer pair of shoes."

"Killer, eh?" He had no idea what that meant, but he was imagining sky-high heels and a very short hemline. Not a very realistic idea, however. "I thought your red one was quite nice."

She crinkled her nose. "That wasn't the happiest night of my life. I've decided to retire that frock to the back of the wardrobe. No, the one I bought is blue and gold. It's very festive."

And because he couldn't curb his curiosity about her footwear he decided to ask. "And your shoes—are they gold as well?"

"Yes. Strappy. With a dangerously high heel."

After the way she'd murmured those words, that wasn't the only thing that was becoming dangerously high. And in the Special Care Baby Unit, of all places.

"And how do you plan to walk in those dangerous heels?"

Her teeth caught one corner of her lower lip for a few seconds before releasing it. "Oh, I don't plan on walking."

Bloody hell. And the dangerously high areas were getting higher.

She laughed as if guessing exactly what he was thinking. Minx!

"I don't plan on walking," she said again. "I plan on dancing."

"Dancing? Well, I hope your dance card is empty, because that is something I would like to see."

Her index finger reached up to stroke across the baby's forehead. "In all honesty, I just want to keep from breaking my neck."

"You seemed pretty competent out there on the ice. Unlike someone else we both know."

"Hmm...you *are* the one who fell, aren't you? Well, as long as you don't take me down with you, we should be fine."

He couldn't hold back the smile. The woman was sexy as hell with a side of realism that made him want to do all sorts of crazy things. "We'll just have to help each other stay on our feet, then."

"I was hoping you'd say that, because if you could see these shoes..."

If she didn't stop talking about them, he was going to have a real problem when he stood up to leave. Time to bring himself back to earth. "Do you think you'll be taller than me?"

"Ha! I don't think they make shoes that tall."

The way she said that made something in his stomach curl. He could have sworn there was a grudging admiration...or maybe even attraction...tucked inside those words.

He might just have to find out.

But not here. Not surrounded by ill children.

Once that Christmas party came around, though, he was going to have to see if the woman was all talk and no action. Or if she'd changed her mind and decided they wouldn't make such a bad pair, after all.

His phone went off, and he glanced down at the screen. It was the maternity unit. "Duty calls," he said. "Can you get her back in her cot without help?"

"I got her out by myself so I think so." She nodded toward the door. "Go on. We'll be fine. If I have any trouble, I'll call a nurse."

With that, Dean climbed back to his feet. But not without throwing one last glance behind him at the woman who was beginning to infiltrate his dreams. And worse, he had a feeling tonight's dreams were going to include a certain pair of high strappy sandals, and, if he wasn't mistaken, he'd be plotting all kinds of ways to get her out of them.

Just then, Jess's phone went off. With a frown, she glanced down at the readout. "Oh, no."

He had his hand on the door, knowing he needed to go. "What?"

"I'm being called down to Maternity as well. It's my friend Amy. I'm her midwife, and she's in crisis."

They arrived in a chaotic maternity unit just as the baby was delivered by C-section. Although the baby was obviously full term, the newborn was blue and limp with no reflexes. No heart rate. The nursing staff were already administering chest compressions. Leaping into action, he went to work intubating the baby and pushing air, while Jess stood in the background looking shell-shocked.

"What happened?" he bit out.

Isabel looked up from where she was still working on Jess's friend, who was under general anesthesia. The floor was littered with bloody towels. "Grade three placental abruption. Worrisome fetal heart rate that bottomed out just as we were going in. We're taking her uterus."

"Oh, God." Jess's startled cry echoed what they were all thinking.

Taking the uterus to save the life of the mother. Even as they worked on the baby, he ached for Jess's friend, who might not only lose this child, but would never carry another.

Fifteen minutes went by in almost complete silence as everyone continued to work at a feverish pace. They administered adrenaline, hoping to stimulate the baby's heart.

"Come on…come on…" He could hear the frustration

in his voice. He realized Jess was standing over him as he willed the newborn to respond.

This time, it wasn't going to work.

Time to call a halt...

Wait. A blip went across the monitor. Then another one. Another.

Everyone paused, staring at the machine, which had gone from almost a flat line to a trio of beats. The jumbled rhythm began to take shape, growing more and more regular with each second.

There! Sinus.

"Keep bagging him. We're getting something."

Jess's voice came from beside him. "I can't believe it."

Abruptio placentae sometimes struck without warning. It was always an obstetrical emergency and depending on the amount of placenta that separated from the wall of the uterus the outcome could be good for both mother and baby, or it could be catastrophic.

"We're not out of the woods yet." They'd have to do an EEG to get an idea of brain function, but his heart was going.

Dean bit out a few more instructions to the team. He was in no rush to move the baby right now. Not until he was a little more stable. Until then, they needed to get him on a ventilator. Dean made the call.

He glanced at Jess. "Are you okay?"

"Amy's my friend. I was going to call her to remind her that she'd missed her last appointment."

"You're her midwife?"

Jess nodded. "She insisted, even though I didn't think it was..." Her eyes closed, and she leaned against his arm.

"She's special to you, and you wanted to be there for her. Neither of you could have predicted this would happen."

She glanced over at the table, where two doctors were still operating on Amy. "What am I going to tell her?"

"The truth. That no one could have foreseen this. It's not her fault. Or yours."

He was a great one for giving that kind of advice. He'd convinced Jess to lie to her parents and sister about their relationship.

To keep her from being hurt.

And why was that? Because of his own past? Because of the way he'd been hurt by his biological family? Jess's case was very different from physical abuse. But he knew from experience that words sometimes wounded just as badly and left terrible scars—scars that might not be visible but that were there just the same.

Jess scrubbed her palms over her eyes. "What if she doesn't make it?"

"Let's not go down that road, yet." He paused. "Does Amy have family here?"

"No. She's all alone. This is her very first baby." She swallowed. "It looks like it'll be her last, if he survives."

He squeezed her shoulder and then released it. "There are other ways. We both know that."

"Yes, but that's not going to make her feel any better right now." She licked her lips. "I keep thinking this could be Abbie lying there. That the baby could have been Marissa."

"But it's not. They're both fine." He glanced back as another doctor came into the room. Within a few minutes, they'd gotten the baby hooked up to the ventilator and orders were written up for the other tests.

"She's going to want footprints made…just in case."

"I'll order it."

Jess's brown eyes were rimmed with moisture. She

drew a stuttered breath. "Thank you. This means a lot to me."

"I'm going with him. I'll let you know as soon as I know something."

"I want to come with you."

"Are you sure you don't want to stay until she's out of surgery?" He nodded toward Amy.

"I can't do anything for her right now." She looked up at him. "Except for this."

They had footprints made as the newborn was rushed from one department to another. When they'd finally gotten him to the SCBU, two hours had gone by.

They went to check on Amy and found Isabel just wrapping things up. "She's still out. We've given her three units of blood," Isabel said. "Who's the next of kin?"

"She doesn't have any that I know of. I'm her friend. I'm listed as her contact person."

They were evidently pretty close friends. You didn't just hand something like that over without a lot of trust on both sides.

With her family the way it was, Dean was glad she had someone to talk to. He'd never even thought to ask about who her friends might be or if she even had any. Maybe because Dean had always been kind of a lone wolf, never really forming those kinds of relationships. Nor had he ever felt the need to.

And judging from the way Jess was hurting for her friend, he wasn't sure he really wanted to. He'd cried into his pillow from time to time at the boys' home after his mum had left. But it was always when no one could see. By the time he was eighteen, the tears had stopped. He couldn't remember a time since when he'd really cried.

Maybe it was a good thing he didn't do relationships.

"You'll let me know if anything changes, right?"

Jess turned toward him. "I'm going to stay with her for a while."

"Are you sure?" Even as he said it, there was something inside of him that urged him to stay as well. Which was exactly why he needed to leave. Now.

"Yes. I want to be here when she wakes up."

And who would be there for Jess?

Not him. It couldn't be. He headed for the door, but just before he went through it, he stopped. Went back over to her. He wanted to kiss her cheek, but the doctors were still there finalizing things. He settled for gripping her hand for a minute. "Ring me if you need me. You've got my mobile?"

She nodded. "Thank you. I will."

As he made to leave once again a part of Dean that was centered squarely in his chest hoped that she would.

CHAPTER ELEVEN

DEAN WAS TALKING to someone on his mobile. Propped against the wall of one of the hallways, he didn't look happy. She couldn't hear the conversation, but he appeared to be doing more of the listening than the talking. Anything he said was short and curt, lips thin, face tight. She started to back away, when his eyes met hers, and he motioned her over.

Great. She'd been on her way to see Marissa this morning. Amy had finally regained consciousness last night and had sobbed in weak, tired squeaks that broke Jess's heart. The baby was still hanging in there, and they'd gotten news that there was brain activity. And the baby was already breathing on his own. All hopeful signs. Even so, it had been awful telling her friend what the doctors had had to do to save her life.

Feeling tired and just a little sad, she made her way over to where Dean was, noticing that he was doing his best to get off the phone.

"I'm not interested in meeting."

His tone was so grim, she wondered who in the world he could be talking to. Had one of his female friends decided to get too clingy and was demanding he turn a one-night stand into something more?

The thought made her cringe, especially after what she'd been thinking of doing.

"Who I'm seeing is none of your business."

Wow. Now that was harsh.

Jess gave a quick wave and mouthed, "See you later," only to have him reach out with his free hand and catch her by the wrist.

"Well, I really wish they hadn't given you this number."

His eyes darkened ominously for a second or two. "You're not my father. You stopped being that a long time ago."

Oh! It wasn't a woman. It was his father. Dean had said his dad had been released from prison and might try to see him. She'd almost forgotten.

What had he been in prison for? White-collar crime? Or something worse? For Dean to say the man was no longer his father, it had to be something quite serious. Or maybe Dean was just angry that his dad had broken the law. He seemed to be a very by-the-book kind of guy. Except when it came to relationships. And lying to her parents.

That still stunned her when she thought about it. She had no idea what had made him step up that day and claim to be her significant other, but he'd done her a huge favor. It had stopped the haranguing and nagging from both her sister and her mother, and those comments about how driven she was by her career.

Which she wasn't. Not at all.

Wasn't she? She'd thrown her heart and soul into her job, going as far as to further train in crisis management—which was why she was often called in on difficult cases. And she was good at her job. She loved it.

But was it enough? She'd thought so once she'd gotten out from under her mum's thumb. But when she'd started in again during their visit, it had made Jess doubt herself.

As did Dean.

Even as angry as he seemed right now, the man was gorgeous. And she could see herself falling for someone like him under the right circumstances.

Which these were not.

"Please don't ring me again." With that, his thumb hit a button on his mobile and evidently disconnected the call. He let go of her hand and dropped his phone back into the pocket of his lab coat. "Sorry about that."

She wasn't exactly sure why he'd called her over there. "That was your father, I take it?"

"Mmm, no. Didn't you hear? I don't have one of those."

Her heart ached to hear the rough edge that still clogged his voice.

"You may not like whatever the man has done, but he is still your dad."

Another sound came from the back of his throat. "Don't think so. And it's probably best not to assume you know him."

That made her blink. "Sorry. I was only trying to—"

He leaned his head against the wall. "Damn it. I'm sorry, Jess. I have no right to take my anger out on you."

"What did he do, anyway, that landed him in prison?"

He turned to look at her. "He put my mum in the critical care unit."

"He what?"

"He hit her. Until she broke."

Her heart froze for a second, and then pounded back into a chaotic rhythm. "God, Dean. I'm so sorry. I never would have guessed. Did she divorce him?"

"I don't know, actually. She left town almost as soon as she got out of hospital."

She swallowed. So his dad had gone to prison, and his

mother had left. How old had Dean been when all of this happened? "Were you grown and gone?"

"Not quite. And I have no idea why I'm telling you any of this. Sorry. I actually wanted to say I'd be happy to pick you up for the Christmas party."

The event was the day after tomorrow, but she wasn't ready to let go of the other subject quite so easily. "Are you going to see him? Your dad, I mean."

This time he smiled. "You don't believe in beating around the bush, do you?"

"You once said I say exactly what I think, so why hold back now?"

"No, I'm not planning on seeing him. Ever."

It was none of her business, really, but something made her say, "Maybe he's changed or wants to apologize for what he did?"

He seemed to mull that over for a few seconds. "It's too late for any of that. If he wants to start his life over, he can do it without me."

Jess could understand exactly why he would say that. She'd tried to do that with her sister at one time. It was why she'd moved away from London, so that she could get a fresh start.

Without the shadows from the past crowding in.

She was still nervous about going to the hotel where her sister had gone into labor. Maybe if she arrived with Dean, it would make things easier.

"I get it. Believe me. And as far as the other subject goes, yes, I would appreciate you picking me up. As long as you don't mind leaving if it gets to be too much."

"Absolutely. We can make a secret sign. When I see you flash it, I'll know it's time."

Something in her heart warmed that he would be willing to do that for her. "What kind of sign?"

He glanced down at her feet. "You said you were going to wear some killer heels. Maybe if you reach down and slide your finger under one of the straps as if they're uncomfortable. It would also make a handy excuse for leaving."

"Good thinking. I like it."

"Great. So how about six-thirty? That should get us there in plenty of time for the buffet line to open."

"Sounds good. You already know where I live."

"I do."

Jess couldn't believe she'd had such doubts about going to the party with him. Now it seemed like the perfect solution.

Except for one thing.

She'd toyed with asking him to go home with her, but he might prefer someone else. She needed to at least give him an out, if he wanted one. "What if you meet someone there that you'd like to get to know a little better? Should we have a sign for that? I mean, I don't want you feeling like you're stuck with me."

"I won't."

Did he mean he wouldn't meet someone he might like or that he wouldn't feel stuck?

As if reading her mind, he slid his fingers under her chin. "We won't need a second sign."

"O-okay." Suddenly very aware of the masculine scent that was weaving through her senses and that there was a nurse at the far end of the hallway, she backed up a step. "I need to get back to work."

Something else popped into her head. "And I'm sorry about your dad. And your mum."

"Thank you, but it was all a long time ago. Water under the bridge, as they say. I need to get back as well. I'll see you Friday evening, if not before."

With that, Dean headed down the hallway, nodding at the nurse as he passed her. Jess turned as well, suddenly forgetting where she'd been going when she'd spotted him. Maybe because she couldn't quite wrap her head around the fact that she was going to the Christmas party with the playboy of Cambridge Royal.

And if nothing else went right for the rest of the day, that was enough to make her smile.

Talk about a prophecy coming true…nothing else went right. Although Amy's baby, Matthew, was still holding his own, three other labors had turned into full-blown emergencies. She'd barely had time to go down and visit Amy and then Marissa. Then Jess's sister had rung in the middle of one of those emergencies and had bullied her way through the system until one of the nurses had pulled her from the room to take the call.

It had not gone well. Jess, at the end of her rope, had almost lost her temper and undone the tentative truce she and her sister had forged.

All she could think of at the end of the day was that the Christmas party had better be pretty damned good. Because she was looking forward to it far too much. And looking forward to seeing Dean in that tuxedo?

Yes. That also worried her a little bit. He'd become far too intuitive where she was concerned, and this little voice inside of her said that she might even be falling for the man. That would be a disaster.

And what about that idea of a fling she'd entertained over the few days? Could she do it and not want more?

That wouldn't happen, because Dean wouldn't let it. So even if she did the unthinkable and got a little too attached, she had him to drag her back to reality. Which was a good thing, really.

She got her bag out of her locker as her shift ended, vowing she was just going to take things one day at a time and see what happened. In the meantime, she had some walking to do. If Dean expected her to be wearing those sexy shoes she'd purchased, she'd better work on breaking them in.

Dean pulled up in front of Jess's house and gripped the steering wheel. His bow tie felt a little too tight all of a sudden. He hadn't seen her since that ugly conversation with his father—who'd tried to ring him several more times over the past day and a half. Dean had let all of the calls go to voicemail. He had no desire to talk to the man. Or to see him.

But he did want to see Jess. He'd never wanted a home or a family, but there was something about her that made him feel utterly comfortable in her presence. Maybe because the woman was who she was. She didn't try to play games or say things she didn't mean—except to her parents, and that was his fault for initiating the whole fake dating thing.

Nothing to do but get out of the car and ring her buzzer. He sat there for a moment longer staring at the cozy little cottage, wondering what Jess was doing right now. She was the punctual type, so he didn't see her still rushing around the place putting last-minute touches on her hair or makeup.

Was she sitting on the couch waiting for him to come to the door? Was she calmly sipping a cup of tea?

She was calm. He couldn't quite picture her losing her temper the way she said she had at her parents' anniversary party.

And yet, she'd gotten angry with him at the pub, so he knew she was capable of it.

Actually, he liked that unexpected flash of fire. Maybe that was what drove her sister to provoke her. There was something satisfying about knowing he could wring a re-action out of her when nothing at work seemed to.

Ridiculous. Why on earth would he want to rattle her?

And why was he just sitting here like a stooge?

He exited the car and headed up to the door. Pressed the buzzer.

As he'd suspected, the door opened almost immediately. And his eyes almost fell out of his head.

She was dressed in a deep blue dress that looked like something a Greek goddess would have worn; the garment was gathered into tiny pleats at her waist with a gold sash. The neckline was bound with the same type of gold edging that went on to form wide straps at her shoulders.

The woman was gorgeous. Beyond gorgeous.

It was quite cool outside, so she must have a wrap of some kind inside the house.

Even as he thought it she opened the door and motioned him in. "I was just finishing a cup of tea. Would you like one?"

Mystery one solved.

Mystery two…her footwear. The long dress covered her shoes, so he had no idea what they looked like. It didn't matter, he'd see them before the night was through, because she'd eventually have to throw him that signal, right?

Judging from the added height, though, they had to be quite tall. He stepped inside. "No, thank you, on the tea, but take your time. We still have half an hour before things really get under way."

"Let me just get my coat and put my cup in the sink, then. Have a seat, I'll be right back."

When Jess turned to head toward the kitchen, his breath stuck in his throat. The band that formed the straps of her dress dropped past her shoulder blades and traveled halfway down her back, before meeting in the middle, exposing a large expanse of pale silky skin.

How could the woman even wear anything underneath it?

You will not look when she comes back.

Of course, when she did, that was the first place his eyes went. Bloody hell. How had he missed that? The fabric was loosely draped over her breasts, but when she reached for a minuscule handbag and a jacket, he caught sight of a distinct pucker.

That meant nothing. She could just have a thin bra on.

Only his body didn't think so. It was coming up with all kinds of interesting images, none of which were doing him any good.

Why did this woman have such a dramatic effect on him? Dean prided himself on being maybe not as cool, calm, and collected as Jess was, but he considered himself a pretty "in control" kind of guy. Maybe because he'd never wanted to be out of control as his dad had been when he'd been drinking. Or feel out of control the way his mother must have felt whenever he'd come home drunk.

Jess blinked at him, a fleeting look of uncertainty going through those brown eyes. "Something wrong?"

"No." He was acting like an ass. "You're beautiful. Absolutely stunning."

Not very poetic, but true.

She curtsied. "Thank you, kind sir." Her eyes swept over him. "You look quite dapper yourself."

Taking the jacket from her, he held it out so that she

could slide her arms through, her scent spiraling up and knocking another cog from his senses.

Suddenly, he had to know. "Have you practiced our signal?"

"I'm afraid I might fall over if I try anything funny in these." With that, she lifted up the hem of her dress and showed him what she meant.

And he could see why she had her doubts. The shoes fit the style of dress she was wearing and made her look tall and lean.

Statuesque. That was the word he wanted.

The sandals were exactly as she'd said they would be, gold with thin straps crisscrossing over the top of her foot and then wrapping around her ankle. To say they were high was an understatement.

He cleared his throat. "Maybe I should be the one making the distress signal." And he could see himself making it right about now. Because he was definitely in distress.

Jess laughed and let her dress fall back down, covering those devastating shoes. "A little different from my no-nonsense hospital gear."

"I'm seeing a wardrobe review in the future once they catch a glimpse of you."

Her hair was caught up in some kind of fancy clip at the back of her head and that streak of gray was on prominent display. He stepped closer and slid the backs of his fingers up the silky strands. "This looks quite fashionable." He loved that little quirk about her. In fact, he loved a few too many things about the woman.

"It only took a minute, really."

And all he could think of was how it would only take a minute to undo the clasp and let her hair fall down around her shoulders in glorious disarray. Or to wake up to find it across his pillow.

He needed to shut down this line of thought right now. Before he decided they didn't need to go to any staff Christmas party. They could have their own little party right here. Right now.

Except he'd already seen what Jess thought of that idea. And he couldn't imagine her settling for less than everything either. She deserved it.

He just wouldn't be the one to give it to her. He needed to remember that. He'd had a phone call that underscored all the reasons why he'd stayed out of relationships over the last fifteen years. He dropped his hand back to his side and took a deep breath.

"Are you ready?"

She nodded. "As ready as I'll ever be."

She handed her coat to the attendant with a murmured thank you.

From the way it was decorated it might have been a completely different hotel from the one her folks had had their anniversary party in. The ballroom was spectacular with arching pillars that shimmered with twinkle lights. Draped satin tablecloths covered the buffet tables, which held a stunning array of food. To the left of the tables, a bar offered up what looked like every type of drink imaginable.

She sent a memo to herself to not go near it. Not because of her grandfather. But because of Dean. He was doing a number on her senses that alcohol couldn't touch. But mixing the two could create an explosion she wouldn't be able to control. And right now, with his hand on the small of her back as he guided her into the room, lighter fluid was slowly being trickled across the kindling in her head. One spark and up she'd go.

Isabel waved to her from across the room, lifting her

glass in salute, but even from this distance her friend seemed a little distracted. Or maybe that was just Jess. And when Dean's thumb found the bare skin just above the back of her dress and skimmed across it for a second, that distraction grew. Then his hand lifted. He leaned down. "Doing okay?"

Was he kidding? She was so far from okay that it was laughable. But there was no way she was admitting that to him. "So far, so good. It looks a lot different than it did during my folks' anniversary party."

That night would never be quite banished from her memory, nor would the guilt, but her sister had seemed a little softer just before she'd left for home—even if they had almost argued on the phone a couple of days ago. Her mum was also a bit more mellow. Whether she had Dean to thank for that or not, she wasn't sure. At some point in time, she would have to set them all straight.

But that day wasn't today. And it probably wouldn't be tomorrow.

Marissa had grown over the last three weeks and was getting stronger by the day. A few more ounces, and she would be transferred to the regular nursery.

So much had happened. Her opinion of Dean had changed entirely. And after hearing him talk to his father... Well, she never would have guessed he'd had such a difficult childhood. He seemed so confident and self-assured as an adult.

His past made her and her sister's squabbling seem petty. And her parents had never hit their children. Mum had been a bit critical at times, yes, but maybe that had spurred Jess's success in her chosen field. And that hard-won calm she was known for might have come from being able to take a step back from whatever was being dished out to her.

"Do you want something to drink?" Dean's voice broke in.

"Tonic water, if they have it."

She smiled, remembering Dean's violent reaction to the drink at her parents' meal. Something clicked into place. "Why do you dislike it so? Does it have something to do with your dad?"

"Hmm." The little humming sound vibrated against her ear. "Yes, actually. I was a little kid who wanted to be all grown up. Didn't quite work out the way I expected."

Her heart ached for him. But his tone had cooled, a clear warning not to pursue this subject any further.

She modified the question she really wanted to ask. "So what *do* you drink nowadays?"

He laughed, sending a shiver over her. "I drink the real stuff. Just to prove I can."

"Since you're a successful doctor, I'd say you have."

"I'll get our drinks. Wait here."

While he was gone, Jess took the opportunity to glance around, feeling kind of out of place. Work was frenetic, and she knew most of these people in a professional sense, but, outside of Isabel, Hope, Bonnie and a few of the other hospital staff, she didn't have a lot of close friends. As if reading her thoughts, Isabel appeared at her side, giving her a quick hug.

"You look fantastic," her friend said.

Isabel was clad in a long green dress that suited her complexion and figure to a tee; Jess returned the compliment. "That dress is to die for. And those earrings... beautiful." Silver chandelier earrings with glittery green stones dangled almost to her shoulders.

"I told you this was going to be a very grown up party."

"No kidding. How did you all pull this off?"

"Teamwork is the key. I had a lot of help."

Jess scrunched her nose. "I'm sorry I haven't been around to lend a hand."

"You've had a few other things on your plate, love, with your sister and niece." Her friend nodded toward the bar, where Dean was currently waiting for their drinks to be poured. "All those rumors are rubbish, aren't they?"

God, she was so glad to be able to tell someone. "Yes. It was a stupid ploy to get my parents and sister to stop asking me when I was going to settle down and have children."

Isabel looked as if she was going to say something and then shook her head. "Just a warning, then. A little batch of mistletoe has been making its way around the ballroom. I've been circling the room to make sure it doesn't find me."

An old flame from Isabel's past had appeared at Cambridge Royal without warning a couple of months ago. She hadn't told Jess much about Sean Anderson, other than the fact that she was dismayed by his presence.

"Did Sean come?"

The other woman's glance darted to the left to the far side of the room, past where dancers floated to the sound of a small chamber orchestra. "Oh, he's here. I'm trying to stay out of his way as well, so if I rush toward you with a look of panic in my eyes, can you stash me beneath one of the buffet tables or something?"

Jess laughed. "Of course I can. You'd just better hope that Sean, the mistletoe and you don't converge at the same place at the same time."

"Not a chance." Isabel shuddered. "I'm keeping my eye on both of them. So far, so good."

Dean appeared at her side, drinks in hand. Isabel greeted him and then turned back to Jess. "Don't forget about that warning. Converging is to be avoided at all costs."

"I won't forget."

Then her friend was off in the opposite direction of Sean, who Jess could swear watched her go when she glanced in that direction.

"What kind of converging are we supposed to avoid?"

"Someone smuggled in some mistletoe, and we're supposed to be watching for it."

One of Dean's brows went up. "And avoiding it, I take it?"

"Yes."

"Would that be such a tragedy? I can remember a time or two when some mistletoe might have been in order." Lazy amusement colored his tone.

Jess squirmed, her face heating. "We didn't have an audience then." Oops, except they had that time at her house. "Well, not one that wasn't planned."

"That's true. And you played your part quite well on that occasion." He handed her the glass of tonic water.

Ignoring his comment, she nodded at the glass in his hand. "What did you end up getting?"

"Whiskey." He swirled the amber liquid in his tumbler and then glanced up with a frown. "It'll be my only one, if you're worried about making it home safely."

"Not worried at all." From what she gathered about Dean's father, he was not angling to be anything like him. "Have you heard from him again?"

"No." He took a quick sip just as the sound of clapping came their way.

Jess glanced to see what was going on and spied the mistletoe being held over the heads of two unsuspecting victims who were being urged to kiss. A quick peck was the result.

"I hope it stays on that side of the room." She took a sip of her water, finding it distasteful all of a sudden. Because of what Dean had told her about his aversion to it?

"What's that face for?"

She laughed. "Just wondering exactly why I've always drunk this. It's quite awful, isn't it?"

"Am I winning you over to the dark side?"

"Maybe the enlightened side."

"Do you want me to get you something else?"

She shook her head. "I'm a lightweight. I'm good with a sip or two, but after that things start going downhill."

"I can't imagine you tipsy." One side of his mouth went up in a half smile.

"It's not a pretty picture, believe me."

Another bout of clapping occurred, still on the other side of the room.

His smile disappeared. "It normally isn't."

She really should try to be more sensitive.

"I'm so sorry your dad hurt you." She touched his arm, trying not to picture Dean as a little boy who was frightened of the man who'd fathered him. "You talked about not wanting me to face my sister on my own. You shouldn't have had to face what he did on your own."

"It's in the past." He held out his drink. "Since you're only good with a sip or two, do you want to share mine?"

Suddenly feeling as if she did indeed need something stronger than her fizzy water, she accepted the drink, letting him take her glass and set it down on a nearby table.

The tumbler was heavier than she expected, and there was an imprint on the side of it—from Dean's lower lip as he'd sipped? A tingle ran over her and, feeling slightly naughty, and very sure that Dean wouldn't realize what she was doing, she turned the glass slightly and drank from that very spot.

God. The smooth whiskey burned her throat as it went down, but it was nothing compared to the scorching heat that went through her when she caught Dean's eyes on her.

He knew exactly what she'd done. She saw it in the flash of awareness in his gaze, the slight flaring of his nostrils. The way his gaze traveled across her throat, and continued downward. Her toes curled in her fancy shoes and panic washed through her.

She was playing with fire. This man was more perceptive—and far more dangerous—than any other man she'd gone out with, including Martin. *Especially* Martin. Dean was an expert at playing these games, while she was a hopeless novice.

But that didn't mean she didn't want to experience what he had to offer at least once. He'd made casual sex seem like the best thing imaginable.

Well, she wanted some of what he was offering, and it wasn't the liquid in this glass.

Feeling a slight dizziness that had nothing to do with liquor, she slowly raised the drink back to her mouth, holding his gaze this time as she took another tiny sip, allowing her lips to remain on the glass much longer than necessary.

Dean's mouth tightened, and he plucked the glass from her hands. "You're going to need that magic signal, Jess, if you keep that up. Only I'll be the one you need rescuing from."

Yes. She wanted that. Wanted to have to be rescued from him.

Dean raised the tumbler to his nose and inhaled deeply, sending another shudder through her. Could he smell her on the glass? Then he drained the drink and set it aside on the table. "Dance with me."

He held out his hand.

She shouldn't. She'd already warned herself that she

was becoming enamored of him. Did she really want to be toyed with and then dumped as Martin had done with her?

No. But she couldn't be dumped if she walked away after one night. No strings. No promises. Just hot sex with the sexiest man she'd ever laid eyes on.

Decision made, she put her hand in his. "Aren't you afraid people are going to talk even more?"

"If they're going to talk, we'd better make it worth their while. We can always set everyone straight later." He drew her against him. "Besides, do you really care what they think?"

No. She didn't. Sure, some of them would gossip for a few weeks, but once she and Dean parted ways the talk would die down, and they'd move on to something juicier.

Placing her hand on his shoulder, she allowed him to ease her onto the floor where others were dancing. This was the second time she'd found herself on a dance floor with him, and it was every bit as heady as the first time. Only this time she wasn't worried about him using her to break some sexual fast, because she was thinking she might like to do a little fast breaking of her own.

With Dean. Who would keep things easy and uncomplicated.

They could probably even remain friends afterward.

Who was she kidding? Stay friends? They weren't even friends now.

Except he'd stepped in and bailed her out when her sister was playing the bully. Had been a great sport when her dad had insisted on evidence that they were indeed seeing each other. If they'd been seriously dating she might even have liked to go out on that hack with him when spring came. Except they weren't, and never would be.

One of her heels tipped sideways for a second, but

Dean immediately tightened his grip, preventing her from falling.

"I told you I wouldn't be doing anything fancy in these shoes."

A low laugh met her ear. "And I knew I would love them as soon as I saw them."

Little pebbles of regret gathered in her stomach. This was what she wanted someday. A partner who would catch her when she stumbled, who would walk beside her through life.

Close your eyes and don't think, Jess. Just feel. That's all tonight is about.

Her fingers slid from his shoulder to the lapel of his tux and curled around it. Just beneath the expensive fabric, his muscles flexed against her touch. Because he liked it?

She hoped so. If this night didn't end with them going back to his place—or hers—she was going to be disappointed. No, more than that, because Dean had been tossing around little innuendos from the time he'd picked her up. Surely all of that word play was geared toward a goal. She only hoped she knew what it was.

Dean turned her, and she opened her eyes to make sure she wasn't about to careen into someone and caught sight of Isabel.

She was standing next to Sean Anderson, and neither of them looked very happy. In fact, when she tuned her ears, she could swear they were in the midst of a heated argument, although she couldn't hear the words past the orchestral music. Just then a sprig of green was placed over the arguing pair's heads, and the rhythmic clapping began. This time she could hear the "kiss her, kiss her, kiss her" coming through loud and clear.

Oh, no! The converging her friend had been so anxious to avoid. Mack Trimble, the male nurse who was holding the mistletoe over the pair with a mischievous grin, received a death glare from Isabel for his trouble, then she turned and stalked away from both him and Sean. Even from here, Jess could see a muscle working in Sean's jaw, but he didn't go after her. He stood there for another minute or two, totally ignoring Mack, who, along with the crowd, realized they weren't getting any satisfaction this time.

Her eyes met Mack's and in slow motion she watched as his brows went up. Horror streamed through her as the man made a beeline toward them.

"We need to get out of here." Jess had barely squeaked out the words when Mack was on them. The shorter man was barely able to hold the sprig high enough to reach over Dean's head. The chanting began anew, people seemingly unfazed by the rebuffing they'd received from their last attempt.

A wave of heat surged into her face and she was pretty sure it had turned bright red. Dean, on the other hand, didn't seem mortified in the least.

"Too late," he murmured. "Maybe we should give them what they want."

"But what about—?"

His lips covered hers, cutting off whatever she'd been about to say. And right now, Jess wasn't even sure what that was.

Vaguely she heard the beginnings of an "oooooooh" from the partygoers because this kiss was no peck and release as most of the other ones had been. Dean's lips remained in place, his fingers going to the back of her head as if meaning to hold her where she was. Ridiculous. She wasn't going anywhere. As surely as electricity held its victim a prisoner of its force field, Dean's sheer presence kept her in place.

The fingers at his lapel tightened until she was hanging on for all she was worth.

Then Dean was gone and the spell broke. A huge ball of laughter went through the ballroom and she realized they'd been kissing long enough to have gathered the attention of a whole lot of people.

Mack, pleased to have gotten so much bang for his buck, bowed and wiggled the mistletoe, pointing it at person after person, only to have them wave him away. A minute or two later, the revelers went back to doing whatever they'd been doing before the excitement started.

She caught Isabel's eye from one of the nearby groups. Her friend mouthed "sorry" and then disappeared, ducking through another cluster of folks.

"I can't believe you did that," she snapped.

One brow went up. "Did you want me to stop?"

Lie. Say you did. That this was a big mistake, and that he needs to take you home pronto.

"I want you to take me home..." There. She did it. She'd gotten the words out. Only there were more consonants and vowels swirling behind the ones she'd released, forming words and sentences that she was powerless to stop. "I want you to take me home and finish what you started."

CHAPTER TWELVE

DEAN'S BREATH RUSHED from his lungs at her words. They were standing in the middle of the dance floor, where he was still reeling from that kiss. Evidently, he hadn't been the only one affected.

And if she was asking him for what he thought she was, Dean was only too happy to oblige. He'd been fighting his attraction for her from the moment he saw her with her niece tucked in her arms, and he was tired of warning himself away from her.

Maybe this wasn't a bad thing. Jess didn't just tickle his lust and then make him want to run as soon as it was satisfied. This was more than that. For the first time in his life, he found himself wanting to make love to a woman and maybe even stick around afterward.

That thought was enough to make his gut clench. Not enough to make him back out, though.

Hell, he couldn't sort all of this out now. That could happen later. Once he got her out of those shoes.

Or maybe not.

Maybe she would stay in them the first time.

He didn't want any misunderstandings about what his intentions were. "If we leave now, it's not going to be for a quick roll in the hay. I'm going to keep you there all night."

Jess didn't bat an eye. "Who said I was letting you leave before I'm done with you?"

The fires he'd banked time and time again flared to life. He touched the toe of his dress shoe to the sandals hidden beneath her dress. "I want the shoes left on."

They were standing in the middle of the dance floor, no longer moving. Instead, they were staring at one another.

Jess smiled. "Then I want yours on as well."

A mental picture of both of them in bed with nothing on but their shoes made him laugh. "Touché."

He threaded his fingers through hers. "Shall we continue our bargaining someplace that's a little more...private?"

"Definitely. Because I have some demands of my own."

His flesh gave a twitch that bordered on painful at that. He was rapidly getting the feeling that Jess's reputation for remaining cool and levelheaded only extended to the workplace. There'd been hints of something simmering below the surface on other occasions. Right now, he was only too ready to find out what that might be.

"In that case..." He towed her through the crowd of dancers not caring that people would talk. They'd been talking about him from the day he'd arrived at Cambridge Royal. For once, they would get it right. He was taking Jess home for exactly the reasons they thought he was. "My place...or yours?"

"Where do you live?" Her words came from behind him.

"Farther out than you do."

"Mine, then."

"I like the way you think." They reached the door and the bellman took his valet ticket, opening the door for them.

"Your vehicle will be here momentarily, sir."

He didn't want to have to wait a moment, or even a second. Nodding at the man, he regretted not being able to go and get his car himself and be on his way.

What was with this sudden impatience? He was normally all about the slow buildup of anticipation. Instead, his skin felt prickly and tight as if he were going to split apart.

She shivered against him. "My coat. I forgot it."

Glad to have something to take his mind off his thoughts, he said, "I'll get it."

He draped his tuxedo jacket around her shoulders and waited for her to slide her arms through it. She then handed him her coat-check ticket. "I'll be right back," he said. Once he was in line, his mobile phone, which he'd muted for the party, vibrated in his pocket.

"Damn." He half muttered the word, wondering if he should just ignore it. What if it was the hospital, though, and something had gone wrong with Marissa or one of his other patients? Not something he was willing to risk.

He pulled the instrument from his pocket just as he reached the coat-check attendant. He handed her the ticket and turned away to check the screen on his phone.

It was a number he didn't recognize. He scrolled through his recent calls to see if he could place it and saw a few more like it. It hit him. It was his father.

His teeth ground against each other. No. He was not going to let the man ruin tonight the way he'd ruined plenty of nights in his childhood. He shut the caller down with the press of a button and then went through the screens until he found the block feature and activated it for that number.

Retrieving Jess's coat and doubly glad they were going to her house in case his father somehow tracked down his address, he noted that his car was finally waiting in front of the hotel. The last thing he wanted was for his dad to show up at his door while Jess was there—or, worse, if he was fresh from a binge of drinking and snogging.

He got outside and accepted his keys from the valet and pressed a few bills in the man's hand. When Jess started to shrug out of his jacket he shook his head, his reasons for being here slamming back through his gut. "I like seeing you in it. Keep it on."

Her smile washed away the last remnants of doubt about doing this, especially when she snuggled deeper into the garment as if she liked the feel of it.

He hadn't lied. He liked seeing her in it. Imagined her wearing his white dress shirt the next morning as they ate breakfast, her nipples just visible...

And thoughts like that would get him into an accident before they'd even arrived at their destination.

He held open the door and waited until she was in before moving around to the driver's side and climbing into the vehicle. "Music?"

She leaned her head against the headrest. "I'm good."

He found his fingers going to her nape, his thumb stroking over that contrasting streak of hair. "I have no doubt of that, Jess."

"How do you do that?"

"Do what?"

"Infuse everything I say with a meaning that makes me want you."

"Do you—" his blood pumped through his veins "—want me?"

"Yes. And I don't want music. Or anything else. I just want to get home and get what you promised."

Maybe the impatience he'd felt earlier wasn't all that unusual, since she seemed just as anxious as he was. The thought reassured him. His one-night stands normally had an expiration date of twenty-four hours. Never before had he gone out with a woman and then waited weeks to sleep with her. That had to be why he felt so off balance right now. As soon as he did this and got Jess out of his system, he'd be fine.

Except he wanted to make one thing perfectly clear.

He started up the car and pressed the accelerator, the powerful motor responding instantly. "I still want the shoes."

"You've got them."

With that, he put his father out of his head and the vehicle into fast motion. He agreed with her wholeheartedly. All he wanted was to get to her house, shut her front door and start doing some of the things he'd imagined doing for the last three weeks.

As soon as her driveway came into sight, Jess breathed a sigh of relief. When Dean's hand hadn't been on the gear shift as he'd maneuvered through traffic, his palm had rested just above her knee, his thumb stroking wicked paths along the outside of her thigh. Her leg was covered by her dress, but it might as well have been bare skin from her reactions. She was sure that he was going to notice her squirming pretty soon as the heat inside of her bubbled to the surface time and time again. In fact, if he'd suggested pulling to the side of the motorway and taking her right there, she didn't think she would have uttered a single word of protest.

He didn't get out right away. Instead, he turned to her, a question in his eyes.

"I haven't changed my mind, if that's what you're worried about."

"Not worried. Just curious."

"About what?"

He paused as if not quite sure how to ask. "About how

your experience with your pickup men went. Was your time with them as easy as you thought it would be?"

It was on the tip of her tongue to shrug and say "of course," since that was probably what he expected. But she couldn't. For some reason, the words just wouldn't come.

So she shook her head. "I wouldn't know."

"I don't follow."

"I didn't go home with either of them. I chickened out."

His fingertips went beneath her chin as he eased her around to look at him. "Why did you pretend you did, then?"

"I thought you might think I was pathetic."

"Pathetic? Never." He leaned over and pressed a light kiss to her mouth. "And since we're baring all, I have to say I'm glad you didn't bring them here."

"You are?" Surprise went through her. She'd thought for sure the truth was going to scare him off. After all, he was looking for exactly the kinds of encounters he'd bet she couldn't have. And he'd been right. At least until tonight. Until the crazy want inside of her drove her to do something so totally out of character that it scared her.

"Yes. Because I want you all to myself, and I don't want you comparing me to those other two men."

She should be insulted. Angry. It was the classic double standard, but she couldn't bring herself to be. Because somehow she didn't think he said that to many women. Did that make her special in his eyes?

She didn't know. And she'd better not care one way or the other, unless she wanted him to take off out of here like a bat out of hell.

Forcing a grin and rolling off the first quip that came to mind, she said, "Then you'll have to compete against my imaginary lover, who sets the bar pretty high."

"Ah, but imagination is nothing compared to the real thing, I promise."

Oh, she had no doubt about that. Dean was going to bring her to explosive heights, if all those little tastes during the last three weeks were anything to go by. And suddenly, she didn't want to wait any longer to see if she was right. "Are you ready?"

"More than ready. I didn't want to leave this house when you came down the hallway this evening in that dress. Maybe I should have just kept you here, instead of going to the party."

If he had, she wouldn't have stopped him.

"Then we need to make up for lost time."

"Sweetheart, no time with you could ever be lost." With that he exited the car and moved around to open her door, retrieving her jacket from the back.

She'd almost forgotten that she was still wearing his tuxedo coat, but had to admit she loved being surrounded by his scent...with the fact that he'd been wearing it all evening.

Fumbling in her little handbag for the keys to her front door, she finally found them, her hands shaking with nerves. How the hell was she supposed to slide it in the lock?

As if sensing her thoughts, he took the key from her fingers and unlocked the door, holding it open for her to pass through.

Once she did, she reluctantly shed his jacket and started to hand it to him, only to have him wave it off. "I won't be needing that."

Gulping, she hung it on a peg by the front door and deposited her handbag on a small entry table. Dean laid her coat over the top of his with a smile. "Seems to be becoming a habit."

"What is?"

He shook his head and then laid his hands on her shoulders, drawing her close. "Being in this house and wanting to kiss you."

With that he leaned down and did just that, his lips sliding over and over hers until she was trembling with need. Still he made no move to deepen the kiss, instead reaching behind her head and plucking the decorative clip from her hair and letting the locks fall around her shoulders.

"Better," he whispered. "Because now I can do this."

He twined a strand of her hair around his finger and something in her belly tightened. No man had ever been that fascinated by her streak of gray before. At least not like this. It was as if he couldn't stop himself from touching it. All she wanted, though, was for him to touch her.

All of her.

So she decided to kick-start things into motion. Reaching up, she tugged on one of the ends of his bow tie, watching as it came undone, her eyes taking in the strong column of tanned skin just above it. His Adam's apple dipped for a second as he swallowed. That alone gave her the courage to push the ends of his tie aside and undo the first button of his crisp white shirt, then the next.

The finger holding her hair flexed, tightening on the locks.

"Jess, what are you doing?" The words were whispered from somewhere above her head.

Smiling, she reached up and nipped his chin. "And I thought you were the experienced one. Or do you normally do this dressed?"

"Not usually. But with you, anything's possible."

The words sent a shiver through her. How was he able to make her feel so special, as if he hadn't done this a million times in a million different ways?

Two more buttons popped free of their holes. A swath of skin came into view, along with a pec that was surprising on a doctor.

More surprising was when he released her hair and grabbed her hands. "I think that's enough for now." He reached down and swooped her into his arms. "Bedroom?"

Looping her arms around his neck, she nodded toward the hallway. "Down there and to the right."

Dean set off in that direction, his strides eating the distance in seconds. He kicked open the door to her room, and she crinkled her nose at the girliness of the space. She'd never identified it as such before, despite the soft colors and a ruffle here and there, but this man's raw masculinity made it seem far more froufrou than it was.

Moving to the bed, he leaned down and laid her on it. She'd expected him to drop her so she'd tensed, waiting for the bounce of the mattress. Instead, he followed her down, his white shirt and black trousers looking out of place against her lavender spread...but in a good way. He went up on one elbow, tracing the skin just above her collar bone. "How does this little beauty fasten? I've been looking for a zipper all night long."

"Y-you have?" The thought that he'd been thinking about how to get her out of the dress the entire time at the party made her mouth go dry.

"I have a feeling every man in that room was looking for the same thing, and damning me to hell for being the one to leave with you."

He was lying. He had to be. The thought that it might be a line he fed to woman after woman made the delicious ache that had been spreading through her belly loosen its grip just a bit.

"I always knew you were a smooth talker."

A slight frown appeared between his brows, and she

thought for a second she might have spoiled things for both of them. "It's the truth, Jess. I don't think I've ever wanted to rush quite as much as I do right now. And yet another part of me is begging me to hold on for as long as possible."

He leaned down and feathered tiny kisses along the skin he'd been tracing a few seconds earlier. "I think a compromise might be in order," he continued. "Think we can satisfy both sides?"

As in doing this more than once? "Oh, yes."

"Zipper?" He came up and stared at her face.

"On the left hand side. It's hidden."

Fingers walked along her hip, heading up until he reached the side of her breast, his thumb strumming over it, but not quite reaching the most sensitive part. He tugged on something. "Ah, here it is."

Down the fastener went in a steady, insistent fashion until it was at the upper part of her thigh. Cool air brushed against her. The same digits that had opened the zipper now ran over the skin he'd laid bare.

She couldn't suppress the tiny moan that welled up in her throat.

As if that sound triggered something, Dean stood, staring down at her as he quickly undid the rest of the buttons of his shirt, tugging it free from his trousers and then tossing it over a chair that was beside the bed. When he went for the fastening on his trousers, she wanted to sit up and take over, but to do that would mean the front of her dress would fall to the side and expose her.

Was that so bad?

So she did it, levering herself into a sitting position, one hand gripping the loose body of her dress and holding it against her.

His eyes narrowed for a second, maybe thinking she was drawing things to a halt.

Nope. Not happening. Not at this point.

"I want to do that," she whispered, eyes on the zipper in front of her. He was hard and ready just beyond that barrier, from the way the fabric bulged to capacity.

"Hmm… I could take that one of any number of ways, but I think we'll leave those delectable options for another time."

With that, he reached a hand in his pocket and pulled out his wallet. "But you can get something ready while I finish what I started." His teeth flashed white as he referenced her earlier words.

He unzipped, leaving her to hold her dress in place with one hand while she flipped open his wallet to try to find what she knew he wanted. Only her glance kept straying up to where he was now toeing off his shoes.

"Jess, you're not trying very hard." His trousers dropped to the floor, leaving him just in boxer briefs—black silky fabric probably designed to help his trousers lie flat. No chance of that, because there was nothing "flat" about him right now. "I think you might need two hands."

Her eyes widened. Just how big was the man?

His chuckle brought her attention back up. "I was talking about the wallet. I think you might need two hands to find what you're looking for."

Oh, Lord, she was such a ninny. Only if she let go of her dress…

It would serve him right.

She let it drop the same way he'd allowed his trousers to fall away. The shoulder straps kept the garment from sliding completely down, but they did nothing to prevent the one side from baring her breast.

Dean's rough intake of breath said he'd expected her

to chicken out. Well, maybe he was going to learn a thing or two about her tonight.

Peeking inside the money compartment, she slammed it closed again when quite a few bills came into view.

"It's there, in the little pocket just below the cards. It's hidden, just like the zipper on your dress."

Jess tried to concentrate, but it was just so hard when Dean was standing there in a pair of briefs and nothing else. He'd already taken off his undershirt and socks.

There! As he said, it was hidden. At first it looked like a row of stitching, but when she rubbed her thumb over it, it separated. She reached in and found a wrapped condom. Disappointment sloshed through her. Only one. And he'd said...

"There are a couple more in the inner pocket of my trousers."

Ack! The smile in his voice said he knew exactly what she'd been thinking.

She could think him presumptuous or any number of things, but right now all she felt was glee. He'd hoped this would happen just as much as she had.

"And now there's the little matter of that dress."

She smiled back up at him feeling like a goon. "And those shorts."

"Then I suggest we do something about both of those. Right now."

CHAPTER THIRTEEN

JESS SAT UP, her hair streaming down her naked back, and all Dean could do was stare.

He was still off balance. His skin still felt just as tight. Sleeping with her had changed nothing.

And yet the woman had rocked his world. More than once. More than twice. He'd slipped a couple of extra condoms into the pocket of his tuxedo, in the wild, unlikely chance that he actually got to make love to her. And that was what it had been. Not that first time. Maybe not even the second. But that third slow, heated rush had sent a bolt of realization through his chest.

He loved the woman.

That was why he'd been in such a hurry. Why even after making love to her multiple times, it still wasn't enough.

Those uneasy sensations weren't going to go away. Not now. Not in two weeks. Probably not ever.

Hell! How could he have let this happen?

Maybe it hadn't been a matter of letting it happen. Maybe it was meant to happen. With her and only her.

Why couldn't he find happiness with someone? Did his upbringing preclude that? Did his father really wield that much power, even now?

Maybe not.

Jess tossed a lock of hair over her shoulder and sent him

a quick glance, blinking in uncertainty at something she must have seen in his gaze. He whisked away his thoughts. He could figure all of that out later. "Are you okay?"

"Okay?"

"Are you feeling all right?" Wow. He was actually at a loss for words. Impossible. It had never happened before.

Then again, he'd never quite been in this position before, where he hadn't tiptoed out the door at the first opportunity.

She wiggled that delectable bottom for a second as if trying things on for size.

He couldn't stop the smile that came to his face. She'd seemed perfectly happy with his size...and with everything else. Those little cries of pleasure, the way she'd gripped his shoulders as he'd moved above her...

Damn, he could have sworn he'd used up every last one of his wildcards, but she was doing something to him all over again. Casting a spell from which he didn't want to wake.

"I'm feeling a little shaky."

Ditto, sweetheart.

He sat up as well and kissed the spot where her shoulder met her neck, a place he'd discovered had the ability to make her arch up. Right on cue, she tilted her head and pushed toward his touch, so he increased the pressure, using the sharp edges of his teeth to scrape across the sensitive nerve endings.

"I have to get up for a minute." She reached across the bed, fingers gripping the dress he'd taken off her.

He circled her wrist with his fingers. "Use my shirt."

His flesh was tightening all over again, and he was all out of condoms. But he wanted to see her slide her arms through his shirt, knowing she didn't have a stitch on beneath it.

She stood, the muscles of her buttocks curving in a way that made his mouth go dry. She pulled the garment off the chair and slid it on. She threw him a look over her shoulder, her delicate brows arching. "And my shoes?"

"On. Definitely on." His voice came out rough and gravelly. She'd indulged him, leaving those high sandals on throughout their lovemaking. When she came back to bed, though, he'd unbuckle those delicate straps and take them off, kissing his way across her arches.

You are in a whole lot of trouble here, Dean.

Maybe he should run out to the nearest local store and pick up some more supplies. But there was a little part of him that was afraid if he left now, she would never let him back in.

And he definitely wanted back in.

If he was going to do this, though, he was going to do it right. And that meant making sure she was as taken with him as he seemed to be with her.

"Next time, then, you have to keep your shoes on," she said.

Dean chuckled and relaxed against the pillows, enjoying watching her totter toward the bathroom, his shirt billowing around the bottom edge of her ass. And since she'd made no move to button the shirt up, he could only imagine what the front of it looked like.

He'd find out when she came back.

And maybe by then he'd figure out how to tell her he wanted more than just one night. Breaking his own hard-and-fast rule about no repeat sex.

He definitely wanted repeats. For as long as she'd give them to him.

Jess was in the shower when the call came. It was Isabel.

"You need to come to the hospital right now."

He sat up. "Is there an emergency?"

"It's your father. He's here."

Damn the man. Couldn't he take a hint? Well, this time he was going to be even more direct. Ugly words came to mind, and he grabbed at them. "Tell him I'm not interested in seeing him."

He was sorry to have to drag his friends into this mess, but he needed to make sure the man understood that he didn't want him in his life.

"Dean." Something in Isabel's voice sent a chill up his spine. "You need to come. Right now."

Her words had him leaping out of bed and looking for his clothes. He could still hear the water running in the shower, but all thoughts of taking up where they'd left off fled. Was his dad drunk again? If so, he should probably have just told Isabel to have the police pick him up and throw him in jail until he sobered up. But he couldn't. Because something inside of him warned him this could be worse. A lot worse.

So much for the man no longer holding any power over him.

He scribbled off a note, telling Jess he'd had an unexpected emergency come up and had to leave. He knew he should knock on the door and say a proper goodbye, but he knew that was what it would be. All the reasons he played things loose and easy came rushing back to him. Not just because his mum and dad had been such train wrecks, but he'd seen what diving into something impulsively could lead to.

Not violence, he would never hit Jess…he wasn't his father. This was about his mum. When she'd left, it had cut him to pieces and left him in a state he never wanted to revisit.

Isabel's phone call served as a chilling reminder of

everything that could happen...of everything that *had* happened.

Thank God he'd never said anything to Jess about his thoughts earlier. If he had...

God, if he *had*...

No. This was how it had to be. He would leave the note. Jess would think he was doing what he always did: playing around and then dashing off. It was better for both of them. And hadn't she said she wanted to see what casual sex was like? Well, this was pretty much how it went.

And right now, he hated everything that went along with it.

He dropped the note onto the bedside table knowing that he needn't worry about her locking him out of the house when he left—because he was locking himself out. For good.

Dean was taking some time off. At least that was what Isabel had said. Jess's emotions ran the gamut. One second she was furious with him. The next, she felt like crying.

She still couldn't believe his dad had committed suicide. He'd parked his rental car behind a building and attached a hose to the exhaust pipe, trapping the other end in the driver's side window. He'd barely been alive when they'd brought him in. But it was only his body—that conglomeration of organ systems. He'd been brain dead. Dean had been the one to ultimately decide to discontinue life support. It had all been over by the time she'd come in to work the next day, thinking the worst and finding it to be true. His note had told her nothing.

Anger swept back over her. After all they'd been through together, he could simply shut her out? Without any hesitation?

Why not? Hadn't Martin done exactly the same thing?

Except she'd believed it would be different for her this time. Somehow.

She'd tried to ring him for hours after she heard the news, but the calls had gone straight to voicemail, and he'd never once rung her back. A week had gone by since he'd left her house…since his father's death and she'd still heard nothing from him.

It would be obvious to any normal person. He didn't want to talk to her.

Why would he? She was no more special than any of the other women he'd been with.

Except she could have sworn…

Shutting down that line of thought, she shifted Marissa in her arms and rocked her, trying to absorb some little measure of comfort.

That was all she wanted to do nowadays. Work and be with this tiny baby. And pray that the hurt would eventually go away.

Please let it go away.

How stupid could she be? She'd done exactly what she'd told herself not to do. She'd fallen in love with the man.

Well, never again.

Dean had told her how he liked his relationships, but had she believed him? No. And here she was, nursing a heart that was in far worse condition than when Martin had left her.

She leaned her cheek against the baby's downy head. "Why can't I just accept it? It's over, Mari."

Not that it was ever there to begin with.

And those shoes? Buried at the bottom of the rubbish bin, where they belonged. She'd chucked her broken heart in beside them. Only that traitorous organ, unlike the shoes, hadn't stayed buried. It had climbed up and out and was now thumping out a painful rhythm within her chest.

But if she was hurting, she could only imagine what Dean was going through. As much as he'd said he didn't want to see his dad, it had to have been a terrible blow to have him go the way he had. Was he feeling guilty? Relieved? Angry?

She had no idea.

Because Dean didn't let anyone in. Ever.

Oh, she might have fooled herself for a moment or two and thought that he was opening up just a crack. The opening had been minuscule, though, not nearly wide enough for a person to squeeze through. And now he'd slammed it shut again.

Was he alone?

Moisture pricked the backs of her lids. The thought that he might be drowning his sorrows in someone else's arms...

A shaft of pain went through her.

"I don't care." She whispered the words to her baby niece, rocking a little harder as the infant continued to sleep. Tears spilled over, and she struggled to blot them with her shoulder before the special-care nurse saw her and asked what was wrong.

She couldn't tell her. She couldn't tell anyone.

Everything had gone according to plan. She'd had a fling with the man, just as she'd wanted. And yet here she sat, gutted, because in the end she'd wanted more from him. So much more.

"Jess?"

She started at the voice that came just over her shoulder. Her head jerked toward the sound, and she found her sister standing there. Abbie took one look at her face and knelt beside the rocking chair. "What's wrong?"

In a totally uncharacteristic move, her sister threaded

her arm through Jess's elbow and squeezed. "Is it Ma-rissa?" She stared at her baby's closed eyes.

"N-no, she's fine." Except the words escaped on a half sob.

"Here, let me take her." The tubes had been removed as Marissa had gotten stronger, so it was just a matter of shifting her into her mum's arms. Abbie sat on the floor, curling her legs beneath her as she held her baby—really held her. She leaned down and breathed her scent as if trying to memorize it, and then kissed her tiny forehead.

This just made Jess's tears come harder. She should be telling her sister to get up off the floor, it wasn't sanitary, but all she could do was stare at them, half in wonder at the change in Abbie and half in pain from what she her-self had lost.

You couldn't lose what you never had. Wasn't that what they said?

Just then, her sister looked up. "I'm so sorry, Jess. For everything I've put you through."

She had no idea what her sister was talking about. "It doesn't matter."

It didn't. Her relationship with her sister was the last thing on her mind right now.

"Is there somewhere we can go? Where I can keep holding her, but get some privacy? I need to talk to you."

The only privacy she wanted right now was the privacy of her own bedroom, where she could sob into her pillows until there was nothing left. Except even that final sanc-tuary had been invaded. Because everywhere she looked, she saw Dean: how ridiculous he'd looked sitting against those ruffled purple pillow shams—and how absolutely wonderful it had been to have him there.

The tears flowed with no signs of stopping. She took a shuddering breath and tried to force back the tide.

"Wait here." Somehow her sister managed to get herself up off the floor, still holding her baby, and went over to the nurse. She must have said something because in a minute or two Abbie was back, and, with Marissa still in her arms, led Jess down the hallway to one of the empty rooms.

Abbie sat on the bed and motioned for her to join her. Jess grabbed a couple of tissues from the bedside table and mopped up her eyes. How pathetic was she? Crying over yet another man who didn't want her?

"Tell me."

Jess looked at her, seeing the dark circles under her sister's eyes, the fact that she wasn't wearing any makeup. Even her hair looked softer and more natural.

She drew herself up tall, knowing the other shoe was eventually going to drop. It always did. Well, this time she wouldn't be drawn into a war of words. She was too tired. Too heartsick. And all of those past problems with her sister were nothing. Nothing, compared to what she was facing.

Sucking in another deep breath, she shook her head. "I think maybe it's you who has something to tell me."

"Okay, then, I'll go first." Abbie hesitated, and then looked her in the eye. "Martin and I have separated."

"What?" Of all the things she might have expected her sister to say, this was not it.

Shifting the baby in her arms, Abbie feathered her fingers across the tiny forehead, down her nose as if she was just now discovering the wonder of the little creature she'd brought into the world.

"I had an affair. Martin was traveling so much and I was sure he was seeing you. I was angry and afraid. It was just going to be the one time. I never meant it to go any further than that. But one time turned into two and pretty soon I wasn't sure what I wanted anymore. Until Martin came home from his trip, and I decided I loved him and wanted to make it work." Her eyes closed for a second or two before reopening. "I broke it off with the other man and thought things could go back to how they were before."

Jess could guess the rest...the reason why her sister had refused to bond with her baby, why she'd been so hateful, throwing those accusations at her at the party. "Then you discovered you were pregnant."

"Yes." Abbie sighed. "I thought I could handle it all on my own. Pretend it was Martin's and that he would never find out. Only it ate me up inside. I was afraid I was start-ing to hate the baby. And then I went into labor at the party, and I almost lost her. That mark on her leg, it was like a permanent reminder of what I'd done. Of what I'd put her through during my pregnancy."

Jess put her hand on Abbie's shoulder. "I'm so sorry. I had no idea."

"I was looking for a fight that night."

"Does Martin know?"

"Yes. I told him. He wants to work things out, but I asked him to move out...told him I needed to come here and see the baby. I need time to think things through."

"The other kids?"

"They're at Mum and Daddy's house."

Jess had to say it. "Martin loves you, Abbie. You shouldn't try to go through this by yourself."

Something swirled in her memory banks, clicking and processing those last words, even as her sister continued to talk.

"I know now what you must have felt like when you found out Martin was cheating on you. I feel like I failed him. So terribly."

Was that what Dean had felt like when he'd discovered

his father had tried to take his life? That he'd somehow failed the man? It was the other way around. His father had failed him. Time and time again.

And now he—just like Abbie—was probably sitting somewhere trying to get to grips with everything that had happened.

Inside her head, the processing finally stopped and a formula appeared. *No one should have to face something like this alone.*

Wasn't that what Dean had said to her when she didn't want to go to the party at the hotel? He'd said she shouldn't have to face it alone. That he would face it with her.

But what had Dean done? He'd done exactly what he'd told her not to do.

"You need to go home. Or, better yet, ring Martin and tell him to come here. I'm sure Mum and Daddy are thrilled to watch the boys. Jerry? Is he okay?"

"He's out of hospital. But after what I did…" Abbie's eyes, so like her own, were wounded and uncertain.

Dean was probably telling himself that exact thing. He'd rebuffed his dad in the hallway, had told him never to ring him again.

There was no way Dean—or anyone—should have to deal with something like that on his own.

Jess needed to find him. If for no other reason than to reassure him that he wasn't to blame for what had happened to his father any more than she was to blame for what had happened to her friend Amy. Somehow she had to make him see that.

She could be his friend. Even if she could never be anything else.

Digging the keys to her house out of the pocket of her scrubs, she handed them to Abbie. "Stay at the cottage. There's plenty of food and supplies. Light a fire and talk this through with Martin. Just the two of you. I won't be there, so it'll be perfect."

"Where are you going?"

"I have a little unfinished business of my own to take care of."

"With Dean?"

She nodded her head, determination growing in her heart. "Oh, yes. With Dean."

CHAPTER FOURTEEN

HE STOOD AT the grave site of his father, the mist from the rain blinding him to everything around him, which was probably a good thing, since he didn't have to wonder if the moisture on his face was caused by the weather or by something else.

He'd made such a mess of things. Not only had he handled things terribly with his dad, but with Jess as well. He'd seen the emergency phone call from the hospital as his sign that things with her weren't meant to be, and that he needed to get the hell out. Yet she was still all around him.

Even here.

He'd purchased a simple grave marker for his father, although he wasn't sure the man deserved it. Maybe his dad had grown to be sorry for his actions. Dean would never really know what had gone through his father's head while in prison, or even in those last couple of weeks of his life.

He should have at least agreed to see him. Hear him out. Maybe then he could have washed him from his system once and for all.

And Jess? Had he done any better with her? He'd taken off, tossing off a casual note in his wake, just as his mum had done all those years ago. And although his thumb had hovered over the answer button on his mobile phone, he'd let her calls go straight to voicemail. Only when they'd stopped coming had he acknowledged the ball of regret that had lodged in his gut with each missed call.

The ball that was now the size of a boulder.

He knelt beside the grave and traced the lettering he'd had inscribed. A name and date of birth and death. No "beloved father" because, in the end, they'd been strangers.

And his mum? Did she house the same regrets? Maybe the time had come to try to find her. He should at least let her know that the abusive man who'd tormented her all those years ago was gone.

And what about Jess? He sat there, not really sure what to do about that.

He loved her. Beyond anything he could have ever imagined. And yet he'd taken off without a word of real explanation.

Didn't he owe her one? To tell her the truth, that he was messed up in the head right now, but that he cared about her? That he wanted to see her again?

She'd probably slam the door in his face—and with good reason, after what he'd done. But he owed her closure.

The kind of closure he'd never been given by his parents. In the end, how did he know his father hadn't tried to give that to him? Unless Dean wanted to perpetuate the kind of negative cycle he'd lived through, he needed to break it once and for all.

His finger dipped into the period at the end of the inscription that symbolized the end of his dad's life. He could at least put a punctuation mark on the end of his encounter with Jess. For both of their sakes.

Unless…

Unless she could find it in her heart to maybe stick with him for a little while. Feel out their relationship. Maybe she could even grow to care about him.

He glanced down at his shirt, water dripping off the end of his chin. But first, he needed to go home and put on some dry clothes. Something in his heart came back to life as he climbed to his feet with one last glance at the small stone below him.

Maybe this wasn't the end. Maybe it was a beginning.

If so, there was only one way to find out.

Jess rang Dean's doorbell one last time. He wasn't home. Scrolling through the personnel records hadn't been the wisest thing to do. She should have just rung his mobile again and left a message asking for a meeting. Except Dean hadn't returned any of her other phone calls, so she didn't hold out much hope that he would return this one.

It was harder to slam a door in someone's face than to ignore a ringtone. At least that was what she'd told herself as she'd pulled into the driveway, trembling with nerves.

The rain didn't help. It wasn't a downpour, but a dreary mist that echoed what her heart had felt over the last week.

Had it only been a week since they'd spent the night together?

Yes. And yet it could have been yesterday. Nothing had changed.

In her way of thinking, Dean at least owed her a straight explanation. Maybe he'd gotten phone calls in the past from other women and had used the same technique, but Jess wasn't other women. She was the one with the reputation for calmly handling difficult situations.

She didn't feel quite so calm now, however.

She felt cold and miserable…and wet.

It appeared Dean's stonewalling might just work, after all.

She'd done a lot of thinking as she drove over here. No woman at the hospital had ever admitted going to bed with the man. So that put her in a different class, because she knew plenty of women who'd leap at the chance to go out with him, not to mention sleep with him.

If she was going to go down, she wasn't going to do so without a fight. Not like some desperate hanger-on, but simply a woman who wanted to hear it straight out: that he didn't feel anything for her and would prefer to leave what had happened between them in the past.

She wasn't going to get that chance right now, evidently. There were no lights on in the house. No car in the driveway. This was something she was going to have to tackle another time. Until then, she'd have to find a hotel or something, because Abbie was at her house probably waiting for Martin to arrive.

Turning around, she flipped the hood of her slicker up and trudged back into the rain, squinting her eyes to keep the water from running into them.

She'd just reached the driver's side door of her little car, when headlights swept into the lane, heading straight for her. The vehicle pulled to a stop behind hers, blocking her exit, but just sat there for a moment or two, engine idling.

What the…?

Then the lights went out and, although it was the middle of the day, she had to squint yet again to help her eyes adjust to the sudden gloom.

The door opened and out stepped the man she'd been longing to see.

Dean.

He looked as damp and miserable as she did, although…

Something. Something in his eyes made the breath catch in her throat.

He slammed the door shut and walked over to her, staring down at her. "You're here."

Trying to place the inflection in his voice, she failed. She had no idea what he'd meant by that. Was he irritated? Well, at least he hadn't said, "It's you. What the hell are you doing here?"

She decided to play it as neutral as possible. "Yes, I am."

"I was going to come find you."

The breath that had been trapped inside of her whooshed back out. He was? Why? She swallowed and then forced the words out. "I was coming to find you."

One side of his mouth went up, erasing a bit of the taut grimness that had been on it a second ago. "You succeeded."

"Yes." Now she was stuck. She had absolutely no idea what else to say. Maybe she should start with what she knew and then move to the questions afterward. "I heard about your father. I'm sorry."

"Thank you. It was a shock. I blamed myself." His smile had faded, and Jess mourned being the one to chase it away.

"It wasn't your fault."

One of his shoulders lifted and dropped, but he didn't respond to her statement. Maybe coming here hadn't been such a good idea. Except he'd said he'd been getting ready to come find her. She had to know why. "You didn't answer any of my calls that day, so what did you want to see me about?"

There was a longer pause this time. Then his voice came through. "It was a mistake for me to leave you that night. I needed you."

Oh, God. Those words were an arrow straight through

her heart—a wonderful piercing barb that exploded into a rainbow of colors, obliterating the gloom. "I'm here now."

Dean took a step forward and wrapped her in his arms. "Yes, you are." His chin came to rest on her head, making her eyes burn.

This was the time. If ever she was going to risk it, it needed to be now. "I need to tell you something."

"Tell me you're not leaving." The words rumbled above her head.

"No. I have no plans to leave, although you may want me to when I tell you what's happened."

"Are you pregnant?"

Was there an edge of hope to those words?

"No. It's only been a week. And we used protection, remember?"

"Protection sometimes fails."

The irony of it struck her right between the eyes. Yes, it did. She'd done her damnedest to protect her heart, to wrap it in layer after layer of latex and shield it from him. Only her attempts had failed miserably. He'd somehow gotten past her barriers and reached inside of her.

"In a way it did." She leaned back and looked into the face of the man she loved, needing to see his eyes when she said the words. "Remember all that talk about casual sex? It wasn't. Casual, that is. At least not for me."

"Not for me either." The smile was back. Wider this time. "I love you, Jess. I don't know exactly when it happened, but it wasn't because of the sex—although that was pretty phenomenal. It was before that."

Jess's throat closed completely, trapping all the words she wanted to say inside of her. Her mouth opened and shut as she tried to force something…anything out.

Dean went on. "A few days after my father died, I realized I couldn't go on shutting myself off from the world, or I'd risk ending up like him. You're the first person I've truly felt anything for since my mum walked out on me all those years ago."

She found her voice. "I love you too, only I've been afraid to admit it. And when you wouldn't ring me back, I assumed you simply didn't feel the same way. That you just wanted me to stop. But I had to hear you say the words."

"Hell, I'm sorry, Jess, for putting you through that." He dropped a kiss on her head.

"Actually my sister was the one who helped me make the decision to come find you."

His arms tightened around her. "Your sister?"

"Yes. We had a long talk. I even brought along my new shoes, since you seemed quite fond of them. I hoped they might sway your opinion. They're in the car. I can get them if you'd like."

He slid to the side and wrapped his arm around her back, then started walking toward his front door. "I don't need the shoes, Jess. Or the dress. I just need you." A wicked gleam came to his eyes. "But first, we need to get you into something dry."

"That reminds me, I still have your shirt."

"I have other shirts. But the dry I'm thinking about is my bed." He paused for a moment when he reached the front door. "We can talk about marriage and rings later. Right now I just want to enjoy walking through every step of the process."

Marriage? He was thinking about marriage?

"I want the same thing."

Dean unlocked the door and swung it open. Then he swooped her into his arms and carried her across the threshold. "But that doesn't mean we can't practice some of the finer points."

As he turned and kicked the door closed Jess wrapped

her arms around his neck, reveling in the fact that this man loved her and she loved him in return. She was looking forward to showing him exactly how much…far into the night and for as long as he would let her.

EPILOGUE

Dean smiled as Jess handed him a large festively wrapped box and then perched on the arm of the couch right next to him. Facing the fireplace—and a Christmas tree brimming with presents—he was surrounded by Jess's relatives. Her mum and dad had come down to spend the holidays with them in Cambridge, as had her sister and her family.

He wasn't used to spending so much time with a group of people like this, but he had a feeling it could grow on him. There'd still been no word from the private investigator he'd hired to look for his mum, but that was something he no longer had to face alone. Jess had been right there with him, every step of the way. Whatever came of it, they would handle it. Together.

Abbie and Martin had evidently made their peace, from the way she was folded in his arms as they watched their children scurry to and fro. Loving touches and the bright glow in their eyes as they looked at each other said things were on the mend. It was the same with Abbie and Jess. Old hurts and irritations would probably surface from time to time, but for now all was peaceful. Marissa had been released from hospital a week ago and was now tucked into a portable cot to the side of the tree, sound asleep. Unlike Jess's nephews, who bounced with excitement over getting the rare opportunity to unwrap presents before it was even officially Christmas.

Tugging the bow on the gift Jess had given him, he marveled at how well things between the two of them had gone. So much so that, despite saying that he wanted to wait on marriage and relish the steps leading up to it, his impatience had gotten the better of him. But that gift—safely tucked in his jacket pocket—would come later, far from the eyes and ears of the rest of her family.

He opened the box and parted the tissue paper inside to find a white dress shirt. When he glanced up, he found her eyes alight with wicked amusement. Over the past week, she'd worn a wide array of his shirts, looking just as mouthwatering in each and every one of them. "I like it," he murmured. "Thank you. I'll have to try it on a little later."

Color swept into her face as she caught his meaning. Because he did indeed intend to try it on—her, that was—as soon as he gave her his own wrapped gift.

He slung his arm around her waist as the kids bounded toward the tree to see who else had a present hidden beneath it. Glancing up, he found her watching him. "Love you," he murmured.

"Love you too."

Jess's parents—especially her mum—seemed a little softer and sweeter as they watched their children and grandchildren laugh and carry on. Their hands had found each other's and clasped tight.

Their happiness seemed in keeping with the holiday, known for its love and gifts.

He squeezed Jess just a little bit tighter, knowing that being here with her was the greatest gift he could ever hope to receive.

It was enough. It was more than enough.

And he planned to savor each and every moment of it, for the rest of his life.

* * * * *

Don't miss the fourth and final story in the fabulous
Midwives On-Call at Christmas series:
Her Doctor's Christmas Proposal
by Louisa George
Available now!

MILLS & BOON®
Hardback – December 2015

ROMANCE

The Price of His Redemption	Carol Marinelli
Back in the Brazilian's Bed	Susan Stephens
The Innocent's Sinful Craving	Sara Craven
Brunetti's Secret Son	Maya Blake
Talos Claims His Virgin	Michelle Smart
Destined for the Desert King	Kate Walker
Ravensdale's Defiant Captive	Melanie Milburne
Caught in His Gilded World	Lucy Ellis
The Best Man & The Wedding Planner	Teresa Carpenter
Proposal at the Winter Ball	Jessica Gilmore
Bodyguard...to Bridegroom?	Nikki Logan
Christmas Kisses with Her Boss	Nina Milne
Playboy Doc's Mistletoe Kiss	Tina Beckett
Her Doctor's Christmas Proposal	Louisa George
From Christmas to Forever?	Marion Lennox
A Mummy to Make Christmas	Susanne Hampton
Miracle Under the Mistletoe	Jennifer Taylor
His Christmas Bride-to-Be	Abigail Gordon
Lone Star Holiday Proposal	Yvonne Lindsay
A Baby for the Boss	Maureen Child

MILLS & BOON®
Large Print – December 2015

ROMANCE

The Greek Demands His Heir	Lynne Graham
The Sinner's Marriage Redemption	Annie West
His Sicilian Cinderella	Carol Marinelli
Captivated by the Greek	Julia James
The Perfect Cazorla Wife	Michelle Smart
Claimed for His Duty	Tara Pammi
The Marakaios Baby	Kate Hewitt
Return of the Italian Tycoon	Jennifer Faye
His Unforgettable Fiancée	Teresa Carpenter
Hired by the Brooding Billionaire	Kandy Shepherd
A Will, a Wish...a Proposal	Jessica Gilmore

HISTORICAL

Griffin Stone: Duke of Decadence	Carole Mortimer
Rake Most Likely to Thrill	Bronwyn Scott
Under a Desert Moon	Laura Martin
The Bootlegger's Daughter	Lauri Robinson
The Captain's Frozen Dream	Georgie Lee

MEDICAL

Midwife...to Mum!	Sue MacKay
His Best Friend's Baby	Susan Carlisle
Italian Surgeon to the Stars	Melanie Milburne
Her Greek Doctor's Proposal	Robin Gianna
New York Doc to Blushing Bride	Janice Lynn
Still Married to Her Ex!	Lucy Clark

MILLS & BOON®
Hardback – January 2016

ROMANCE

The Queen's New Year Secret	Maisey Yates
Wearing the De Angelis Ring	Cathy Williams
The Cost of the Forbidden	Carol Marinelli
Mistress of His Revenge	Chantelle Shaw
Theseus Discovers His Heir	Michelle Smart
The Marriage He Must Keep	Dani Collins
Awakening the Ravensdale Heiress	Melanie Milburne
New Year at the Boss's Bidding	Rachael Thomas
His Princess of Convenience	Rebecca Winters
Holiday with the Millionaire	Scarlet Wilson
The Husband She'd Never Met	Barbara Hannay
Unlocking Her Boss's Heart	Christy McKellen
A Daddy for Baby Zoe?	Fiona Lowe
A Love Against All Odds	Emily Forbes
Her Playboy's Proposal	Kate Hardy
One Night...with Her Boss	Annie O'Neil
A Mother for His Adopted Son	Lynne Marshall
A Kiss to Change Her Life	Karin Baine
Twin Heirs to His Throne	Olivia Gates
A Baby for the Boss	Maureen Child

MILLS & BOON®
Large Print – January 2016

ROMANCE

The Greek Commands His Mistress	Lynne Graham
A Pawn in the Playboy's Game	Cathy Williams
Bound to the Warrior King	Maisey Yates
Her Nine Month Confession	Kim Lawrence
Traded to the Desert Sheikh	Caitlin Crews
A Bride Worth Millions	Chantelle Shaw
Vows of Revenge	Dani Collins
Reunited by a Baby Secret	Michelle Douglas
A Wedding for the Greek Tycoon	Rebecca Winters
Beauty & Her Billionaire Boss	Barbara Wallace
Newborn on Her Doorstep	Ellie Darkins

HISTORICAL

Marriage Made in Shame	Sophia James
Tarnished, Tempted and Tamed	Mary Brendan
Forbidden to the Duke	Liz Tyner
The Rebel Daughter	Lauri Robinson
Her Enemy Highlander	Nicole Locke

MEDICAL

Unlocking Her Surgeon's Heart	Fiona Lowe
Her Playboy's Secret	Tina Beckett
The Doctor She Left Behind	Scarlet Wilson
Taming Her Navy Doc	Amy Ruttan
A Promise...to a Proposal?	Kate Hardy
Her Family for Keeps	Molly Evans

1215 GEN STD LP

MILLS & BOON®

Why shop at millsandboon.co.uk?

Each year, thousands of romance readers find their perfect read at millsandboon.co.uk. That's because we're passionate about bringing you the very best romantic fiction. Here are some of the advantages of shopping at www.millsandboon.co.uk:

* **Get new books first**—you'll be able to buy your favourite books one month before they hit the shops

* **Get exclusive discounts**—you'll also be able to buy our specially created monthly collections, with up to 50% off the RRP

* **Find your favourite authors**—latest news, interviews and new releases for all your favourite authors and series on our website, plus ideas for what to try next

* **Join in**—once you've bought your favourite books, don't forget to register with us to rate, review and join in the discussions

Visit **www.millsandboon.co.uk**
for all this and more today!